ANCHOR

doubleday

new york   london

toronto   sydney   auckland

CONCRETE CANDY

stories

apollo

AN ANCHOR BOOK
PUBLISHED BY DOUBLEDAY
a division of Bantam Doubleday Dell Publishing Group, Inc.
1540 Broadway, New York, New York 10036

ANCHOR BOOKS, DOUBLEDAY, and the portrayal of an anchor
are trademarks of Doubleday,
a division of Bantam Doubleday Dell Publishing Group, Inc.

Library of Congress Cataloging-in-Publication Data
Apollo, 1980–
Concrete candy: stories / Apollo.
—1st anchor books ed.
    p.   cm.
     1. City and town life—United States—Fiction.
2. Inner cities—United States—Fiction.
3. Afro-American teenage boys—Fiction.
4. Teenagers' writings, American. I. Title.
PS3551.P53C66   1996   95-35288
813'.54—dc20   CIP

ISBN 0-385-47780-5

BOOK DESIGN BY TERRY KARYDES

Contents

TO MY BRUTHA JESS
FOR ALL THE ENCOURAGEMENT AND O.E.
AND FOR MOM—WHO ELSE?

CONCRETE CANDY

Four Wolves and a Panther

Jamie sat with the Wolves around him in an abandoned West Oakland warehouse. Its windows were smashed, and the crumbling brick walls were covered with graffiti and gang tags. Jamie was thirteen and a street kid. His parents had kicked him out because they were afraid that all his black friends and black books were turning him . . . black. He was only ten then, but as quickly as he was kicked out Jamie found a new family called the Wolves.

They weren't a gang, but if the police or media found out about them they probably would have said different. The name, Wolves, came from THE JUNGLE BOOK.

The Wolves sat around Jamie, smoking and laughing and sharing a forty-ounce Colt. Leon studied Jamie long and hard.

"So why you talkin all this 'I wanna be black' shit, man? You known us long enough to see that don't mean nuthin!"

At sixteen, Leon was the oldest Wolf. His hair was a wild Afro, but tamed now by a gray bandanna. His skin was midnight, his body muscular. His nose was flat, lips full, and his eyes as amber as a real wolf's. Those eyes were fixed now on Jamie as he sucked at a hand-rolled cigarette.

Jamie was white, but the many days spent in the sun had polished him gold. His hair was long, tangled brown, and reached his mid-back. His eyes were an emerald green that sparkled with a touch of sunlight. He almost never wore a shirt, but today he wore a huge yellow, red, and green tee. He was slim but padded with muscle. A cigarette smoldered between his fingers, its glowing point dripped ash.

"I know it don't mean nuthin! I just FEEL black . . . like . . . like under my skin." Jamie sighed, staring down at the dirty concrete floor. "The last time I seen my dad, he made this big deal about not recognizin me."

Leon looked at Jamie and smiled. He brought the cigarette to his lips. "It take 'sponsibility to be black. And it take heart to say shit like that."

A chubby little chocolate-brown boy sitting in the corner giggled. He wore his hair in a fade and had a snub nose, chubby cheeks, and pouty lips. His dusk-colored eyes were friendly, and his jiggly stomach was a roll of puppy fat. At eight he was the youngest Wolf. "Hey, man!" he called to Jamie. "Why don't you do a Michael J., 'cept reversed."

Jamie almost laughed, but Leon turned to the boy. "Shut up, Little Jay."

The third Wolf was an ebony boy of thirteen. His hair was styled in baby dreads and his nose was small and bridgeless. He had buckteeth, and a gold ring glinted in his left nostril. He was awkward and slim and called Black Fang, but just Fang saved time. He sat beside Little Jay, sipping from the bottle of Colt .45 and listening to Jamie and Leon.

The last wolf was twelve, tall, skinny, and the color of

old city soot. His eyes were a lionlike gold, and his hair was combed back and matched his eyes. It was funny: you never imagined a brother with hair that color, but Matt's definitely was. He sniffed the stale air in the building, and his nose wrinkled.

"Yo, man! It gettin stuffy in here. Can we talk about this shit outside, Leon?"

Leon stood up and looked out through a space where a door should have been. Morning rose into noon. "Matt be right. Let's walk some an 'cuss this."

Jamie peered up at the sagging ceiling as he followed the other boys out to the baking street. "This place so old we be lucky it don't fall on us!"

Little Jay laughed, walking beside Fang and Leon. "This Oaktown, man. What you spect?"

Now on the sidewalk, the five boys walked together, Jamie beside Little Jay, and Leon, Fang, and Matt beside him. Fang passed the Colt to Jamie, who took a swallow and handed it to Leon, who finished it off. Leon turned to Jamie.

"So you really wanna be black, huh? I mean, white folks think most of us wanna be white, not the other way around."

Little Jay tugged at Leon's arm. "Well, Jamie ain't really white."

Leon smiled but said nothing. Jamie cocked his head.

4

"Man, I always had respect for black dudes, y'all know that for a fact. Never really consider myself as white. An, like I said, on the inside I feel like I'm as black as you, Leon. Just wish I could see how it is to be black on the outside too."

Little Jay looked at Jamie thoughtfully. "Um, I read this book, writed by a writer who was a white dude, an he took these pills that made him black."

"You can't read," Jamie said.

Little Jay fingered his jaw, then spread his little brown palms. "Okay, so my mom read it to me. Shoot bullets through me. So how come you don't buy some Black-O-Matic pills, man?"

Jamie pushed a long tangle of hair away from his face and patted Little Jay's shoulder. "We ain't got no money to 'ford that shit."

Leon tightened the bandanna around his head and looked up at the skyline of ramshackle buildings as he rolled a cigarette. "Well, brothas, sound like this a serious thing Jamie talkin. How 'bout we go on to my place an 'cuss this over a pizza an some more Colts?"

A little while later at Leon's apartment, all the boys were gathered on the couch, their stomachs full of pizza and Colt .45. Leon took a last sip of malt, lit a cigarette, and looked over at Jamie. "Talk to me, man. So you really wanna be black, huh?"

Jamie shifted pizza crust in his mouth and talked around it. "Shit yeah, man!" He watched Little Jay plow through a pizza slice.

"But why?" asked Fang.

Jamie frowned. "Why what?"

"Why you really wanna be black?"

"Oh. Well, I spose I've always felt that way . . . but if you wanna get real technical bout it, spose it started when I was four or five. I got real sick and had to go to the hospital . . ."

Jamie was interrupted by Little Jay's laughter. "Now he tellin ole-time stories!"

"Shut up an let him talk, dude!" said Matt.

Little Jay stood up, put his hands to his hips, and his lips formed a pout as easily as they would a smile. "Make me, sucka!"

Little Jay charged, and wrestled Matt to the carpet. Now sitting on Matt's chest, he snagged a fork that had fallen to the floor and held it up in the air. "Little Jay, the warrior! King of Oaktown!"

Matt gasped for breath, struggling to get the eighty pounds of eight-year-old off him. Leon scowled at the two boys. "Both y'all stop with the lil-kid shit! Sit your asses back on this couch an listen to Jamie!"

"Okay," Jamie began again. "So I real sick in the hospital. I shared a room with this black dude, bout my age. He had that disease called . . . um . . .

what you call that disease only black people can get?"

"Rodney King disease?" muttered Fang.

Leon scowled. "Mean, like, sickle cell?"

"Um, yeah. That it. Anyway, while people were givin me balloons an all kinds of shit, nobody was givin him nuthin. I used to go over to his bed and talk to him and give him my balloons an toys. It was . . . like we was CONNECTED in some way . . . like we knew each other from . . . BEFORE!" Jamie looked up at Leon and the other Wolves. "That sound dumb, man?"

Leon smiled. "Naw. That totally cool."

Fang gulped Colt. "Yeah. Word, man."

Jamie looked down at the floor. "I feel like I can FEEL other people's pain, mostly. Whenever I hear somethin bad happen to blacks, like by some white dogfuckers, I feel so bad. I gots a ebony skeleton an a real-black soul!"

"Well, man . . ." Leon squeezed Jamie's shoulder. "WE see you just as black as all of us."

Jamie looked at Leon and smiled. Little Jay waddled over to Jamie. "Wow! You 'member back when you was four?"

Everybody cracked except Jamie and Leon.

"Naw. My mom told me. A long time ago."

"Um, before they kick you out, huh?" Matt asked.

"Matt!" Leon shouted, and punched the boy's shoulder.

apollo

"Aw, it's cool, man," Jamie said. "I don't care 'bout them no more. Shit! THEY the ones who kick me out . . ."

Jamie reconsidered. "Well, technically I left. Man, y'all dudes met my parents when I was still livin with 'em. I was black an they was just white trash! They hated me! One time I even had this dream where I WAS black an in a shop shinin this sucka's shoes. I looked up at his face an it was my dad!"

Leon looked thoughtful. "Mmmm. I got a idea. Jamie, go into the bathroom an sit on the toilet."

Jamie frowned, but went into the bathroom.

"Matt! Get the big, sharp scissors. Fang! Get the 'lectric razor."

All the Wolves stood in the bathroom. Matt held the scissors, and Fang had the razor, and Jamie's frown deepened. "What you doin, Leon?"

"Yeah, man?" Little Jay added.

"Makin you black."

"Huh?" asked Jamie.

"Matt. Cut most of his hair off. Fang. You shave the rest with the razor."

Matt nodded and began to cut Jamie's hair.

"The fuck you doin?" Jamie yelled.

"I said, we makin you black!"

Jamie clenched his fists, feeling his hair get shorter. "Man, Leon, if I look stupid after this I'll . . . I'll . . ."

Leon just grinned and watched Matt cut. Finally, Matt

was finished. Brown locks filled a Kmart bag, and Jamie looked down into it with disgust. His hair didn't even reach his ears now.

Leon looked over at Fang. "Shave, man."

Fang nodded, and the razor buzzed. Jamie looked up at him. "Better not cut me, asshole."

Fang and Little Jay laughed as Fang began to shave. Leon grinned, arms folded as he watched. Jamie looked pissed as hell, and Little Jay's mouth just hung open in fascination. Now the only hair on Jamie's head was little brown prickles. Jamie looked a little less pissed now, but still not happy. Leon sat down and looked at Jamie with approval. Fang went and put both the scissors and the razor away.

"So what you think?" Leon asked Jamie.

Jamie brushed his hand over the prickles. He frowned, but then smiled a little. "My head's shaved, but I'm still white!"

"Ahhh, but we ain't finished yet." Leon fumbled through the cabinet and brought out what looked like a brown bottle of peroxide. "This some kinda skin dye shit my mom got last year. It supposed to be for dyein black people's skin if you got white spots like Michael J. claim he had. Anyways, we paint you with this shit you be black for least a week."

Little Jay looked confused. "But your mom black ALREADY, Leon!"

Leon frowned. "Well maybe she wasn't black enough! Shit, how I know?"

"Um, you gonna PAINT me?" asked Jamie.

"Just wiggle out yo' clothes, dude," Leon said.

Jamie's clothes dropped to the floor, and he sat naked on the cold toilet lid. Leon got three small sponges from the dye kit. He gave one to Fang, one to Matt, and kept the last one. Little Jay frowned. "Hey! What 'bout ME?"

Leon smiled and patted Little Jay's shoulder. "Sorry, little bro, but I don't think Jamie would want you messin up his blackness."

Jamie squirmed a bit as Leon began to expertly paint his face with ebony dye. Leon painted his whole head and added another layer. Matt and Fang did just as good on his legs and feet and arms and hands. A feeling of excitement rushed through Jamie as they painted, and he squirmed once more. He was going to be black!

"Stop wigglin, man!" Fang snapped.

"Well, excuuuuse me!"

"Y'all keep paintin," said Leon as he stroked Jamie's neck with the sponge while Matt carefully dabbed at a nipple. Finally Leon put the sponge down and blew air tiredly. He stepped back and studied Jamie.

"All right. Your upper body all done. Fang almost finished with your legs."

Jamie saw the amazement on everyone's face, and gazed up at Leon. "How I look, man?"

"Mmm. Well, you look black, except your unfinished legs."

"Cool."

Fang knelt back down and gave Jamie's legs, feet, and toes another coating. He painted with long strokes, concentrating hard. "Finished," Fang said finally.

Everyone gathered closer to Jamie, who glistened ebony.

"Whoa!" said Little Jay.

"Cool!" added Matt.

And finally, "You look total good black," said Fang.

"I do?" Jamie asked. "Um, can I look now?"

Leon nodded. Jamie carefully got up and went to the full-length mirror in Leon's room, Fang, Matt, and Little Jay following. Jamie stood in front of the mirror and looked at his naked self.

"Wow! I'm . . . I'm . . . I'm really black!"

Leon smiled as Jamie dashed back into the bathroom. "Thanks, Leon!" He hugged Leon, but then pulled away. "The stuff ain't gonna rub off, is it?"

"Naw. It dry now."

Jamie looked puzzled. "What 'bout my green eyes, man?"

Leon grinned as the other Wolves came in and sat down. "Oh, well, it ain't really noticeable, but for some reason it make you look more black . . . sorta like that panther on the coffee ad."

"Uh, guys?"

Everyone turned to Little Jay.

"How 'bout we still the Wolfs, an Jamie the King Panther?"

Leon nodded. "Yeah. That would be cool, man. Well, now that Jamie's black we should take him on a little tour so he SEES how it is to be black . . . On the outside. Any ideas?"

Jamie looked up at him as he pulled his jeans back on, followed by his shoes and his Rasta-colored T-shirt.

"How 'bout Hilltop Mall over in Walnut Creek?" Fang suggested.

"Yeah. That sound cool, but it gonna be closin pretty soon, so we gots to hurry."

The Wolves left Leon's apartment and piled into his black van. Soon, on the other side of the Caldecott Tunnel, the van pulled into a parking space in the mall lot, and the boys got out. Like a pack of wolves, they followed Leon.

As the boys walked through the crowded mall, their shoes squeaked on the spotless Pine-Sol-scented floor. It was clean and white, while the boys were black and dirty. Jamie watched white people stare at him and the other Wolves like they had just come from another planet, or more likely shipped over from Africa. Some stares were looks of pure hatred, too ignorant to see past the skin to the soul. As Jamie walked behind the rest of his friends, he saw a white lady rush her kids out of the way to let them pass. Her face was a mask of fear. Other white people looked at them with disgust, probably wondering what a bunch of niggers wanted at their mall.

Leon's voice interrupted Jamie's thoughts. "We gonna go to the bathroom. All these dudes gotta piss. Um, you cool, Jamie?"

"Yeah. I wait."

Jamie walked around the mall some more. White kids backed away when they saw him coming. They were afraid of him because of his color. He walked a little more and bumped into a tall, thin white man and felt cold green eyes staring at his skin. He looked up at the man's face. It was pink, with a gray-brown mustache under a wrinkling nose. His hair was brown and cut short. Jamie recognized him, and his mouth dropped open. The tall, worn-faced man was his father!

Jamie was speechless as his father's eyes traced over his ebony skin. There was a strange look on the man's face, and Jamie read it easily: confusion. Jamie's dad frowned, and he looked at the green-eyed black boy staring up at him.

"I seen you somewhere before, kid?" he mumbled.

Jamie said nothing, but slowly shook his head. His dad's eyes narrowed.

"Move, nigger boy."

Concrete Candy

"C'mon, dammit!" Zebra yelled, tailing his skateboard and turning to look back at his friend.

Squirrel came rolling fast, kicking hard, one hand behind him as usual to hold up his drooping SilverTab jeans.

"Can't we just fuckin rest a while, man?" Squirrel panted, skidding to a stop and brushing the sweat from his forehead.

Zebra smiled. "I wish, man! Seem like nobody gots time to rest no more! Anyways, wanna be late for school again? Like it always sayin on TV . . . 'it very cool to follow the rules.'" Stomping the tail of his board, Zebra flipped it into his hand. It was a Steadham Street; curved nose, curved tail, Powell 85 wheels, and skull graphic.

Squirrel stepped off his board and picked it up. It was about the same size as Zebra's, but was a Frankie Hill. Like Zebra, Squirrel rode Venture trucks but had Spitfire wheels. "Ax me, there gettin to be more rules every day," he muttered. "An, once more people start knowin they rules, less people wanna follow 'em!"

Zebra placed a foot on his board and got ready to deck. "Well, if you don't get your ass on your deck an follow ME, we both gonna get tardies up the wazoo!"

Just turned fourteen, Zebra was an average-sized boy with a hint of baby chub padding muscle that would begin to harden in a couple more years. His mother was black and his dad was white, though the man had checked out before Zebra had a chance to know him. Zebra's skin was a deep, wild-honey color that seemed to change shades when the sun went down. He had a high-cheekboned face, a slightly snub nose, and golden eyes that, like his skin, seemed to change at times and become dark and fierce.

His hair was done in long ratty dreadlocks that flowed down his shoulders and back. Zebra was a quiet boy who usually kept his thoughts to himself . . . except when hanging with Squirrel.

Squirrel was also fourteen, and the boys had been homeys since kindergarten. Squirrel was black like dusty charcoal; a chubby, sweet-faced dude who could also be the world's worst wisecrack. He had those kinds of lovable cheeks that grandmothers liked to pinch, his nose was wide, and his teeth were large and usually peeked out from under his heavy lips in some sort of smile or grin. His street name, Squirrel, fit him naturally and he liked it a lot better than his real one: Sydney . . . especially since Zebra had given it to him when they'd first met. Despite his big bobbing belly, Squirrel was fast and could kick ass on his board. His Paris T-shirt stretched over his stomach like a sloppy coat of paint, and his Nikes were so worn and ragged that one big toe stuck out. Squirrel had worn a fade for a couple years, but was going back to his roots with a bushy Afro barely tamed by a battered black White Sox cap.

Zebra rolled his Steadham back and forth with his foot and wiped sweaty palms on his faded purple jeans. "Well, c'mon then. Let's motor." He kicked off with one dirty white Reebok. Squirrel tugged his pants up and quickly followed.

Ten minutes later, the boys tailed to a stop in front of

their school. Squirrel moved close to Zebra as they climbed the steps. "Hope the doors ain't locked yet."

The security guard was just locking the doors as the boys reached the entrance. He looked pissed, but jerked out his key and kicked the doors open. "Y'all late! What you been doin? Hangin in the hood?"

Zebra sighed. "You gotta have a death wish if you wanna hang in THIS hood!"

Squirrel made a face at the man as they passed through the metal detector in the front hall. "Sorry. We had this major crack deal goin down!"

The guard glared. "Why, you little smart-mouthed . . ."

Squirrel cupped his hand over his ear. "What? I'm goin deaf, speak up, sonny!"

The guard looked pissed as hell. "Why, I oughta kick your little no-good . . ."

"Yeah? Well, I oughta sue your ass for . . . for . . . hittin me an shit!" Squirrel suddenly spun around and dropped his jeans. "See? Told ya I had crack!"

The guard's face twisted. "Get to CLASS!"

Squirrel hitched up his jeans. "Jeez! You gonna have a fit?"

The guard jabbed a finger at the hall. "GO!"

The boys moved through hallways still swarming with kids. Teachers' voices carried from classrooms, mostly yelling for order. Finally, the boys pushed through a door numbered eleven and into their first-period English class. It had already started. The two homeys slid into their seats at the rear of the room, slipping their skateboards underneath.

"Well, Zebra, Syd . . ." The teacher began.

Squirrel gave her a hard look.

"Oh, excuse me, SQUIRREL and Zebra. Nice you two decided to come!"

Squirrel smiled sweetly. "Yeah, in my pants, Mrs. Hooper."

The teacher's scowl deepened as snickers and giggles rippled through the room. Everyone knew Squirrel was the class clown, and most teachers didn't want to waste time going one-on-one with him.

As if on cue, a big white cop entered the room.

Squirrel rolled his eyes. "Musta got word 'bout my crack."

The teacher ignored Squirrel. "This is Officer Strapp from the Oakland Police Department. He's here to speak with us about the DARE program. He'll be here all day, so feel free to talk with him at breaks and at lunch period."

Squirrel groaned. "I think I gonna be sick."

Zebra frowned. "Oh, shut up! What you got against cops anyways? Just give him a chance. Maybe he's different."

The cop walked to the front of the room. His black uniform fit almost perfectly, as if it had been made for him, but you could see the slight bulge of a bulletproof vest beneath his shirt. The scents of shave lotion and gun oil trailed after him. He stepped to the podium like he owned it, trying to make his hard eyes friendly. Zebra watched the man, almost expecting his face to crackle like broken glass when he smiled.

"As your teacher has told you, I'm Officer Joe Strapp . . ."

Squirrel's hand went up, and the cop forced a smile. "Yes?"

"So," Squirrel began, "you're one of those good cops, right? You don't go round beatin people? . . . How you like Rodney King, man?"

Strapp's face flushed pink. "That's not important right now!" He tugged at his shirt collar. "Questions at the end of our session, please." Going to the blackboard, he wrote "DARE" with a piece of red chalk. "Now, I'm sure you all know that DARE stands for Drug Awareness Resistance Education . . ."

Squirrel leaned close to Zebra. "Always thought it meant Drugs Are Really Expensive!"

Zebra poked him. "SHUSH, fool!"

The teacher scowled. "Do you have something you'd like to share with the class?"

Zebra sighed. "No, Mrs. Hooper."

Strapp eyed the teacher and began again. "DARE was

started about eight years ago by Bay Area police officers. We go to inner-city schools and . . ."

Squirrel glanced at the cop's gun belt, and his hand shot up again. "Hey! How come you can bring guns to school an kids can't?"

The cop grinned. "Police officers are allowed to carry guns because we need to protect ourselves."

"So do kids, but WE'RE not allowed to carry guns!"

Strapp tugged at his collar again. "That's another matter, son! . . . And we are having questions at the end of class!" He turned to the board. "As I was saying, DARE was started about eight years ago by Bay Area police officers. We go to various school districts and spend five to six months educating children about drugs and violence. We'll talk to you about all the different kinds of drugs from marijuana to crack cocaine, about the effects of each drug, and how to avoid them . . ."

"The effects?" Squirrel asked.

"No! The drugs!" The cop frowned at Squirrel. "Attitude is a very important survival tactic in this area."

Zebra's hand went up. "Wouldn't it be simpler to stop the drugs from coming into our cities, instead of going to schools and talking about them?"

Strapp spread his palms. "There's really nothing we can do. Tons of drugs come into the U.S. on big ships and planes every day."

A girl raised her hand. "Yeah? Well, so do Haitians, but the U.S. has no trouble keeping TONS of them out!"

The cop's face reddened again. "I'm not here to talk about Haitians, young lady!"

Zebra's eyes went hard. "Why can you find shiploads of Haitians but can't find shiploads of drugs?"

Squirrel snickered. "I bet he could find shiploads of doughnuts!"

The cop slammed a fist against the blackboard. "Drugs are already IN your neighborhoods! You kids are using them and spreading them around!"

Squirrel waved a casual hand. "YOU'D probably be smokin concrete candy too if you lived in this hood!"

"What's that?" Strapp demanded.

Several students twisted their caps backward and stared out the window.

"Crack, fool!" snapped Squirrel. "Duh! I thought you was a expert!"

"SQUIRREL!" Mrs. Hooper yelled, leaping from her seat. "I've had just about enough!"

Squirrel twisted his own cap around. "So have I," he mumbled.

Officer Strapp cleared his throat. "Please bear with me, kids. I'm here to teach you about these drugs . . ."

Squirrel rested his chin in his hands, staring boredly at the cop. "Yo! We could learn more about drugs by using the fuckin things than what you've taught us so far!"

The cop clenched his hands on the podium. "Police are here to HELP you!"

"Sure!" Squirrel shouted, above the other rising voices. "Just like Dr. Kevorkian!"

"SQUIRREL!" yelled Mrs. Hooper. "OUT! NOW! Go stand in the hall!"

Squirrel stood and strutted across the room, his chubby frame stopping in the doorway. "'Tude is veeery important!" he muttered."

The cop glanced from the clock to Mrs. Hooper. It was as if he couldn't wait to leave. He gazed around the room and saw pairs of black and brown eyes all challenging his icy blue ones. He adjusted his collar once more and spoke. "Now," he began, his voice coming out raspy. "You kids are the future. I want to hear from you."

Zebra watched Squirrel leave the room. "I think you already have!"

"ZEBRA!" Mrs. Hooper shrieked. "One more comment and you can go join your friend in the hall!"

Zebra crossed his arms over his chest. "You don't gots to tell me! I go my ownself!"

The cop blew out air. "Sometimes the things police officers have to do must seem a little harsh to you guys."

One more kid turned his cap backward. "What y'all did to Rodney King seemed a LITTLE harsh!"

"He probably had the wrong attitude," muttered Zebra.

"OUT!" shouted Mrs. Hooper.

Zebra got up and headed for the doorway. "You don't gots to tell ME twice!"

The cop's face flushed once more. "If you have a gun . . ." He paused and glanced around the room. "You can turn it in and you'll receive a pair of tickets to a concert of your choice."

"Why don't you turn yours in!" Zebra yelled from the hall.

Squirrel stood by the water fountain, sucking a grape Tootsie Pop. "You was a little harsh on that cop, Zee."

"He ain't got a clue."

Squirrel peeked in the doorway. "Maybe that why they sent him here."

The school day passed by quickly. Squirrel and Zebra walked along the sidewalk in front of their school. Their shirts were tied around their waists, and they carried their skateboards by the front trucks. Suddenly the cop came storming down the steps.

Squirrel smiled at him. "Um, OFFICER Strapp, are you still available?"

The man clenched his fists and pursed his lips. "Yes."

"What happens with all those guns that been turned in for concert tickets?"

"They're destroyed, of course."

"Gee. Then where do you get all your throwdowns?"

The man's pale face went crimson. Spinning on his

heel, he stalked away. "Fucking zoo!" he muttered. "Nothing but a fucking ZOO!"

Squirrel dropped his hands to his hips, spat in the street, and stared after the cop. "Know what? Your attitude sucks!"

Zebra touched Squirrel's arm. "Chill, man. Maybe the dude is trying to help, but don't know how. I mean, remember the cop that came last year? He was pretty cool."

"Yeah. But he was also black, ready to retire, an born an raised in Acorn district of West Oakland!" Squirrel shrugged. "Well, maybe he is tryin to help, but he better clean up his attitude."

"Aw, c'mon, let's cruise by Burger King. Um . . . who payin?"

Squirrel smiled. "Guess you are, homey. Y'know, It's Wednesday, an my mom be runnin short."

Zebra ruffled his dreads. "Ain't nobody's mom be runnin LONG in this hood! But I got a few Washingtons. Let's go."

Squirrel slapped his stomach. "That my man!"

The boys were both sweat-sheened by the time they reached Burger King. The shabby restaurant was jammed between two buildings that looked about ready for the wrecking ball. The gray sky threw a dull glaze over everything.

Zebra and Squirrel slipped their shirts back on before

entering the King. It was packed with kids from Zebra's school, and he nodded to a few that he knew. Then he and Squirrel made their way to the counter.

"I have me a Whopper an fries, an a mega-Coke," Zebra said to the young white girl behind the register.

Squirrel shoved Zebra aside. "I take TWO Whoppers, a fries, an hella orange soda!"

The cashier looked puzzled, and she turned to check the menu behind her. "HELLA? Does that mean large?"

"Naw," said Squirrel, grinning. "It mean hella, just like you Daisy Dukes, girl!"

The cashier looked more confused than ever. "My what?"

Squirrel's grin widened. His big teeth flashed, and dimples formed in his cheeks. "Your a . . ."

"It mean large," Zebra said quickly, giving Squirrel a poke in the roll of chub where another boy's ribs would have been.

The cashier still looked puzzled, but handed the boys their tray of food.

Zebra scowled at Squirrel as they went to find a table. "Yo! Why you gotta go around stirrin up shit all the time?"

Squirrel looked thoughtful as they took their seats. "Ain't it weird how no matter where we go, we always take seats at the back of any place? Maybe it in our blood?"

Zebra took a bite of his burger and washed it down

with a sip of soda. "Huh? . . . Aw, just shut up and eat your lunch!" He looked pissed and tore into his food. "Man, you play too fuckin much! One of these days you gonna get capped. THROWDOWNS!"

Squirrel waved a hand. "Aw, that fool didn't say nuthin in class today!"

Zebra popped the last bit of burger into his mouth and frowned. "That cause you didn't let him talk!"

Squirrel crunched ice with his teeth. "Yeah? Well, you wasn't so polite to him neither!"

"Well, least I gave him a chance!"

Squirrel burped. "If he do really wanna help, he better start preachin the solution instead of the prob!"

It was just after three, and Squirrel and Zebra stood in front of their school. Kids burst out the doors and into the street.

Squirrel glanced at his homey carefully, trying to figure if he was still pissed. "Um, got a cig?"

Zebra reached into his jean pocket, pulling out a pack of Camel Lights. "Sure." Both boys took one and Zebra fired them with his Bic. He took a small hit and blew smoke. "Taste good after a meal, huh?"

Squirrel nodded, blowing sloppy smoke rings. "Figure we gettin hooked?" He studied the cigarette between his ebony fingers. "Tobacco a drug too, y'know."

Zebra shrugged and took another puff. "You wanna get technical, so's orange soda. I don't think splittin a pack a week gonna ice our asses." He pointed at the street. "What round here probably gonna do us a lot quicker." He thought for a moment. "White people on TV always sayin how cigarettes are real bad for you, and how we should try an get rid of 'em. Well, I spose they right, but crack's REAL bad for you too, an it seem like ain't nobody tryin to get rid of that." He paused and looked at Squirrel. "Sometimes it seem like they figure we just monkeys, man. It like somebody out there . . . call 'em zookeepers . . . they think all kids stupid. Like, we can't see the lies they feed us every day."

Squirrel stomped out his cigarette and giggled. "Aw, that cool, Zee. I didn't inhale! So's now I can be President, huh?"

About three hours later, the boys were sitting on Zebra's ragged couch in his apartment. The window was open, and the light coming through had that rosy, kicked-back glow of evening. Both boys were barefoot, their feet resting on the coffee table as they finished their home-work assignments. Almost together, they flipped away their pencils, which bounced off the wall and landed on the carpet. Squirrel yawned and stood up. He patted his stomach and went into the kitchen. "Got anything to eat? It way past my feedin time."

Zebra stretched. "Um, there some frozen pizza we could nuke."

"Way cool!" said Squirrel. His jeans slipped low on his

hips, but he didn't bother pulling them up because he felt at home at Zebra's. "Yo! I gonna have me a beer first. Want one, Zee?"

"Well . . . Okay, but if my mom find out we been drinkin again, she have a cow for sure!"

"Yo! We score some more later! She never know."

Zebra frowned. "Beer ain't easy to score, man. Not like rocks!"

Squirrel shrugged. "We could always shoulder-tap." He ripped two beers from the sixer and tossed one to Zebra. Returning to the couch, he plopped down on the cushions. Both boys popped the tabs and drank deeply. Zebra studied his can for a moment. "Coors ain't that good."

Squirrel chugged his beer. "Well, least it cold. So maybe we score some Olde English. That kickin!"

"Naw, it gots to be Coors again, 'member?"

"Why she buy this dog piss anyhow?"

"It on special. Why else?" Setting his can on the table, Zebra stood and clicked on the TV.

Squirrel killed his brew and burped. "You gonna nuke that pizza while you up?"

Zebra nodded and glanced out the window before going into the kitchen. Night had come to Oakland. Things were happening in those streets that the boys were aware of but didn't want to think much about. It was better to be safe in Zebra's apartment, watching reruns of THE

SIMPSONS and eating microwave pizza. A few minutes later Zebra returned with the pizza. It lay piping hot on a platter. Squirrel plowed right in, sucking down pizza slices like a vacuum on mega-suck.

"Want another brew, homes?" Squirrel asked, squirming to his feet.

Zebra took another sip from his can. "No, you go ahead. Three ain't gonna be no harder to score than two, I guess."

Squirrel opened the fridge. "Don't eat all the pizza."

"Jeez, Squirrel, ain't you worried about gettin so fat?"

"Why? They pass a law against fat too?" Squirrel returned with the beer. He settled down on the couch, sinking into its nap. "Yo! Maybe I be one of those Sumo dudes when I grow up. I hear they make a shitload of bank!"

Zebra sipped beer and smiled. "Ax me, you more likely be a hippo when you grow up."

"Mmm." Squirrel thought a moment. "Maybe I slinging concrete candy." He gulped his beer. "Get my grip on that way."

Zebra made a face. "What you on?"

Squirrel burped again. "Life."

"That original." Zebra said, and ate one more pizza slice. He drank the last of his Coors, and clicked off the TV. "After you done we best bail over to a liquor store and see about scorin some more beer."

Squirrel stretched and stood. "Aw, we gotta go now? RUGRATS be comin on next."

Zebra slid into his jacket and snagged his skateboard. "Yeah. It gettin dark an my mom be home soon."

Squirrel stretched and stood. "We gonna miss X-FILES too."

Zebra smiled and headed for the door. "Well, we probably see some sorta ghost on the way there." He gazed out the window. "It 'bout time for them kinda people to come out."

The boys walked out into the hall and descended the stairs to the sidewalk. The evening air was chill with a salty breeze that blew in from the bay. The streetlights had just begun to come on.

"So how we gonna score this time?" asked Squirrel. "Find us a winehead?"

Zebra considered. "That usually work, but I think it be easier if we motor down to that new store. That ole Korean guy was pretty cool last time we was there."

Squirrel shrugged. "Yeah, but he just hungry for biz. Plus, in this hood, you either friendly or get capped!"

Zebra smiled. "Well, you was pretty cold to that cop an you ain't caught no bullets."

Squirrel flipped Zebra the finger.

The boys decked their boards and rolled down the street. As the sky got darker, more zombies came out of doorways and burned-out buildings. They begged for quarters from Zebra and Squirrel, but the boys continued on, cutting into the parking lot of a little corner store that had a bright neon sign glowing on its peeling front. The building next to it was only a crumbling shell, and a kid voice called out from its gaping black doorway.

"Yo, brothas!"

Both Squirrel and Zebra tensed, and cautiously turned around. A tall, thin, dark boy, maybe fifteen or sixteen, stepped from the shadows. He wore new Machine jeans, huge new Cons, and a Snoop T-shirt. His hair was done in fret braids, mostly hidden by a white A's cap turned backward. The boy held out an open hand, revealing the usual packet of sparkly powder. "Yo, brothas, take it. This here a sampler."

Zebra made a face. "Fuck off. I got my own sugar at home."

Squirrel giggled, spun around, and dropped his jeans. "Yo! Here's MY crack, sucka! An it just say no!"

The kid looked surprised, but smiled once more. "Yeah? Well, this crack FREE!"

Squirrel shrugged and pointed to a woman standing on another street corner. "So's yo' mama, boy!"

The dealer boy gave Squirrel a dirty look and then glanced around, seeming unsure. He peered at Zebra in the fading light. "You a Rasta mon, huh? Yo! Check it. I sell you a blunt!" He slipped the crack packet into his jeans pocket, replacing it with a sloppily rolled joint, fat with weed. "This here some good strong shit! Straight from Humboldt County! Get ya closer to Jah real quick!"

Zebra fingered his dreads. "Just cause I wear these don't mean I wanna fuck the mind JAH gave me! Rasta symbolize peace, not just gettin high! An PEACE be why I wear dreads."

The dealer kid shrugged and put the joint back into his pocket. "I don't need a lecture from some little hood rats what don't count!"

Squirrel patted his chest. "THIS little hood rat got his-self a AK at home! THAT put you Jah's lap, sucka! Reeeely quick!"

The dealer boy's hand dropped to the pocket of his baggy jeans once more, this time bringing out a shiny .357. "Well, I gots this HERE, dick-face! Bullshit walks, but you better RUN before I get in a bad mood!"

Squirrel opened his mouth, but Zebra quickly grabbed his arm. "C'mon." He glared at the dealer boy. "Don't waste time on shit what don't count!"

Squirrel spat on the concrete, barely missing the boy's spotless shoes. He picked up his board and followed his homey toward the liquor store.

Zebra chuckled as they entered the doorway and the sensor bonged. "AK! Ain't no future in the front, man."

Squirrel shrugged. "So I lied! Sue me!"

"I tell you one thing, homey, if that dealer found out you been bullshittin 'bout everythin, he'd do somethin way worse than sue ya!"

The inside of the store was brightly lit and carried the scent of fresh paint. No posters of models or beer advertisements plastered the walls yet, and the coolers and shelves were only about half stocked. It must have been hard to start a new business when there were two other liquor stores on the intersection's other corners. There was no one else in the place. The Korean man looked up from a tiny TV behind the counter and smiled at the boys. His smile dimmed a little as Zebra went to the cooler and selected a sixer of Coors, and his smile fully disappeared as Zebra carried the Coors to the counter. But then the man smiled once more.

"Young man make . . . mistake?" he suggested.

Squirrel looked up. "No, it for his mom. See, she LIKES Coors!"

Zebra spread his hands. "Really she don't, but it on sale. Good price."

The man cocked his head. "Yes. Sale. But not for you."

"Yeah," said Zebra. "It ain't for me. It for my mom."

The man glanced around the empty store and then out the doorway at the equally empty sidewalk. "For . . . mother?"

"Yup," Squirrel said. "We can't stand the stuff."

The man looked confused, but reached under the counter and brought out a sixer of Coke. "We . . . trade?"

"Um," said Zebra. "N-ooo. But . . ." He reached to his pocket and slapped a ten-dollar bill on the countertop. "Here. Take this. All of it!"

The man just peered at the money for a long time. "All?"

"His mom likes you," added Squirrel. "Want you to stay in business."

The Korean's eyes shifted from the ten-dollar bill to the doorway. Quickly, he bagged the sixer and took the money. "Next time bring note from mother."

Zebra and Squirrel exchanged glances, then bowed from the waist. The man hesitated a moment, then smiled and bowed in return. The boys left the store.

Outside it was totally dark. Squirrel decked his board. "He's cool."

Zebra shrugged, rolling the top of the six-pack sack to grip it before decking his own board. "Guess it like you said, he need biz."

Squirrel's eyes flicked to the burned-out storefront where the dealer boy still lurked in the doorway. "Guess everybody need biz, huh?"

"That ain't business; that called bein a house nigga! C'mon. We best cross to the other side of the street."

The boys were halfway down the block when a police

car came cruising up behind. It cut to the curb in front of them, but its siren hadn't screamed and its strobe light didn't flash. Instead, its spotlight blasted a blinding beam straight into their faces. The boys tried to shade their eyes, Zebra shifted the sack to his other hand and squinted to see a big figure step out of the car. He recognized the voice immediately.

"Hello, boys. Isn't it a little late for you to be roaming the streets?"

Squirrel grinned. "Well, if it ain't good ole PATROLMAN Strapp. Too bad you ain't a B-ball player! Then you'd be a jock!"

Zebra gave Squirrel a poke in his chubby side. "We just been shoppin for my mom."

The man switched off the spotlight, leaving the boys almost blind in the dimness. He stepped close, drumming his fingers on his gun belt. "What exactly were you buying for your mother?"

Zebra glanced at the bag, then at Strapp. "None of your business! An anyways, it ain't no drugs, so why should you care? You don't give a shit 'bout anythin else!"

"Yeah!" Squirrel piped, pointing to the dilapidated building where the dealer waited. "You want drugs? Go check him out! Fool slingin concrete candy! Better get backup, cause he gots hisself a three-five-seven too!"

Zebra could see the dealer kid huddle as far back

from the doorway as he could. But Officer Strapp put his fists to his hips and stepped in front of the boys, blocking any chance for them to roll away. "We're dealing with alcohol right now, boy. And alcohol is a drug. You are minors possessing it! You're breaking the law."

Zebra glared at the cop. "How you know it alcohol? You think just cause we young and black we automatically got alcohol?"

A slight smile came to Strapp's face. "Do you realize that if I arrest you and your friend right now, you could have the process of getting your driver's licenses delayed until you're twenty-one and you could spend up to six months in jail?"

Squirrel snorted. "What 'bout that fucka across the street?"

"We're not over there, boy. We're right here! And I'm not talking to him, I'm talking to you! Just give me the beer and go home."

Sudden anger shot through Zebra. "You don't care about no law! You . . . you just want some goddamn free beer!"

The big man moved fast. He whipped his club from his belt and hit Zebra hard on the side of the head. The bag slipped from Zebra's hands and he crashed back into the wall of a building, then slowly slid down to the sidewalk.

"FUCKA!" Squirrel yelled. He almost leaped at the

cop, but Strapp raised his club and Squirrel shrank back. Then the man returned the club to his belt and picked up the sixer. He got back in his car.

Squirrel spat. "See you in school, you dick-suckin liar!"

Officer Strapp popped the tab on one of the cans and chugged beer. "Who's going to believe you, nigger!"

The car squeaked away down the street. Squirrel forgot about the cop and sank to his knees beside Zebra, who was sitting up against the building. A trickle of blood ran down his cheek.

"Zebe!" cried Squirrel. "You okay, brotha?"

Zebra nodded. "A little dizzy but I live, man. Maybe even long enough to worry 'bout my goddamn driver license!"

From across the street came the dealer boy's laughter.

Bad Boyz

"Jamar! How many times I gotta tell you! Clean up that room of yours!"

Jamar sighed and made a face. "I ain't got time for that shit, Ma! I goin out!"

Jamar's mother stormed into the kitchen. She wore a baby-blue bathrobe, and pink curlers decorated her hair. "Y'all goin straight to hell, boy! That the only place you goin!"

Jamar scowled. "If I can take Oaktown, I can take hell! Any black MAN could! . . . But I ain't your BOY! An you can't send me to my goddamn room no more!"

His mother glanced at the small wall clock: it was a smiling Mickey Mouse, and its white-gloved hands stood at 8:13. "Everybody get the hell they deserve, boy." She poured herself a cup of coffee. "Seem like a MAN would have enough pride in himself to clean up his own mess."

Jamar aimed a finger at the clock. "You gonna be late for work, Ma."

His mother sighed. "Nice of you to worry about me an my work once in a while. Ever think of getting your own-self a job?"

Jamar picked up his bowl of Froot Loops and sucked down the remaining milk. "Shit! Ain't never gonna catch me workin my ass off for chump change in no Burger King!"

His mother shook her head. "Well, you gone an drop out school. What else you gonna do?"

"School for KIDS, Ma. I ain't a kid no more." Jamar got up, leaving his empty bowl on the table. "I got 'portant shit to do. MAN stuff!" Jamar walked out of the apartment, slamming the door behind him.

Jamar was eighteen, six feet tall, and solid muscle. His skin was the color of chocolate, and his hair was done neatly in big braids. His clothes were all new: huge Karl Kani jeans, dark blue sweatshirt, and big-buck Nikes. He crossed the sidewalk and headed for his car; a new Plymouth Neon, jet black. The Crips had given it to him in payment for a job . . . a MAN'S job! It even had a phone.

Jamar started the engine, then opened the glove compartment. Inside was a .38 special with ivory grips, lying atop a dark blue bandanna. He pulled out the bandanna and tied it around his head, then flipped the compartment shut and slid a Master P disc into the CD player. Slamming the gas, he burned away from the curb, the hard rap echoing after him as he sped down the block.

He idled the car to a stop at a red light. The phone beeped in its cradle. He picked it up. "Yo."

The voice on the other end was deep but friendly. " 'S up, J-man?"

"Oh. Hi, Razor. Just kickin it. What up wit you?"

"Hangin. Wanna meet me an Zombie front of A&B Liquors?"

The light changed, and Jamar stepped on the gas once more. "Everythin cool?"

"Chillin. But there some shit what need dealin with."

Jamar swung the car around a corner. "See ya in a few, man."

Five minutes later, Jamar pulled the Neon into the

liquor store parking lot and cut the engine. Two figures stood in the shadows against the store's side wall. Jamar slid from the car and walked over to them; Razor and Zombie. He flashed the Crips sign.

Razor was tall and lean, mud brown, with eyes like old asphalt. His teeth were large and his hair red-tinged. A blue bandanna encircled his head, and his black leather jacket was a little too small. He offered Jamar a forty-ounce of Olde English.

Jamar took a long chug, then wiped his mouth. "So, whattup, Razor?"

The tall dude glanced around. "Word say . . ."

A silly-sounding giggle interrupted him. "Word s-say them red-rags b-b-been messin where they don't b-belong."

Razor glared at the other dude beside him. "That what I was gonna say, stupid!"

Jamar shook his head. "Y'all fucked again, ain't ya?"

Zombie just grinned and giggled some more. He was small, and his hair was a matted mop like a whirl of untended dreads. Though seventeen, he had the uncalculating face of a child and, like always, seemed surrounded by a mist of crack smoke. A little pipe, dead now, hung loosely from his lips.

Jamar studied the dude a moment more, then frowned. "Put that shit away, man. That smell makin me sick."

Zombie only giggled again. "S-sure never b-bother ya when you was s-s-sellin it!"

Jamar's frown deepened. "I moved up since then. Why I wanna keep sellin to little kids?"

Razor glanced at Zombie, then frowned at Jamar. "HE was just a lil ole kid when you started sellin. Look what YOU made him."

Jamar jammed his hands in his pockets and turned away. "Aw . . . He a man now, he should know better!"

Razor sighed. "Anyways, some Bloods jump one of our boys at Richmond BART yesterday. An as Eazy-E say, 'It time to pay the paper!' You handle a drive-by?"

Jamar made a face, then smiled. "Y'all forget who you talkin to, nigga? Course I can! Now THAT a real man's job!"

Razor smiled a twisted smile. "Good. I got a Uzi full-auto on loan for ya!"

Jamar gave Razor the brother shake. "A man's gun for a man's job! . . . Um, I gotta do this alone?"

"Naw. I'm sendin Zombie along."

Jamar scowled. "Shit, bein wit Zombie just as good as bein alone! Last time me an him done anythin, it was jackin little kids for bags on Trick-or-Treat night."

Razor shrugged. "Be like ole times! . . . 'Cept now you get to kill kids 'stead of just takin their candy."

Jamar glanced at Zombie again. "Well, okay. So when this sposed to happen?"

"Tonight. Friday always good for drive-byin. Five-O busy runnin their asses all over town. The red-rags usually be hangin outside Khan's Klub. I send Zombie round your place 'bout eight with the gat."

"Okay. Um, what these guys look like? They be in colors?"

Razor shrugged. "Zombie tell ya."

Jamar nodded, then glanced at Zombie. "I see you later . . . an stop smokin that goddamn rock so much!" He started for his car.

Zombie just grinned and fired his pipe.

The sun had set and darkness was settling over Oakland. Jamar stood on the sidewalk outside his apartment building, leaning against the Neon and smoking a Kool. He sighed and glanced at his Casio watch: 8:13. Zombie still hadn't shown. Jamar tossed his cigarette on the concrete and watched its ember die. Then he tensed at the sound of footsteps coming toward him. He gripped the .38's butt and turned. He let out a sigh of relief at what he saw: two boys about twelve, scrawny and small. One had a shade of skin that shone like honey under the streetlamp, and the other was so dark that Jamar could hardly make him out against the night sky. The boys froze when they saw Jamar, and he could sense their fear. They quickly began walking past him.

"Yo!" said Jamar.

Both boys turned. "Yeah?" the honey-colored kid said.

Jamar frowned. "Don't 'yeah' ME, boy! What your friend got in the bag?"

The dark boy stepped in front of the other, offering his brown paper bag. "Um, c-cookies . . . we sellin cookies for school."

"So's we can go on a field trip," the second boy added.

Jamar considered. "Gimme one."

The dark boy handed Jamar a box of Double-Mint Fudge cookies.

Jamar tore open the box and ate a cookie.

The dark kid puffed his little chest. "Hey! They two dollars!"

Jamar grabbed the boy by his shirt and jammed the .38's muzzle against his chest. The boy's legs sagged and tears softened his ebony eyes. Jamar smirked at the boy, knowing he was paralyzed by fear. "Your little hood-rat life only worth two dollars, boy. You wanna lose it?"

Both boys gasped, and the dark one shook his head. Jamar let him go and they ran off. Jamar laughed, then slid the gun back into his pocket.

The smell of crack fumes thickened the air and made Jamar's eyes water. Zombie came walking over, his thin frame bulked by a huge parka. He opened the jacket to reveal a big black Uzi.

"Get your ass in the car!" Jamar growled, snatching the Uzi.

Zombie grinned his little-kid grin. "Hey, cookies! Can I have one?"

"Yeah, just get your ass in the car!"

Zombie wobbled over to the Neon and got in the driver's seat. He loaded his pipe and fired it.

"Shit!" muttered Jamar, sliding into the passenger seat and slamming the door. "Can you drive while you smokin that shit?"

Zombie grinned. "S-shit, if I can walk an s-s-smoke, drivin can't b-be no harder!"

Zombie started the engine and stepped on the gas, blasting the car down the block.

Jamar checked the Uzi, making sure the clip was in place. Then he cocked the bolt and flicked the select-fire switch all the way forward to "A."

Zombie began to sing as he drove. "It's a b-b-beautiful day in the neighborhood, it's a b-beautiful d-day in the . . ."

"Shut up, Zombie."

"You s-said I could have a cookie."

Zombie swerved the car around a corner and slowed in front of a shabby nightclub. There were about ten guys standing outside. Three leaned against the stucco wall, sharing a forty-ouncer.

Jamar cranked down his window and stuck the gun

muzzle out as the car neared the curb. "Zombie! Which ones?"

Zombie pointed. "The ones wearin red! D-duh!"

Jamar felt sweat break out under his shirt. "They ALL wearin red, fool!"

Zombie looked again. "The three d-dudes s-s-sharin the forty."

Jamar steadied the Uzi, then jerked the trigger. The big gun bucked in his hands. Orange muzzle flame licked out toward the three figures on the sidewalk. He saw the bodies jerk and spin as bullets ripped through them. Blood spurted onto the sidewalk and the nightclub's wall.

Zombie skidded the car around the next corner, then floored the gas.

Jamar shoved the smoking Uzi under the seat and wiped sweat from his forehead. "Shit! Stop at that liquor store. I need me a drink."

Zombie pulled the car into the liquor store parking lot. Jamar got out and walked toward the building, a small wooden shack with windows smothered by beer and malt posters. There were two neon signs in the window: one pink and reading "C&C Liquors," and the other yellow, saying "OPEN." Both flickered half dead. Inside it smelled like Clorox and Garfield air freshener. The man behind the counter was Korean, and wore a silk button-down and a gold chain. He watched Jamar from the corner of his eye as Jamar went to the beer cooler. Jamar took two fortyouncers of Olde English, then walked to the register, glancing once at the surveillance camera as it swung away from him.

The Korean man frowned. "You no buy! You under age! Store closed! Go!"

Jamar scowled. "If the store closed, you best turn off your 'open' sign!"

"Get out my store!"

Jamar flipped him his fake ID. "Say twenty-one here, don't it?"

The man peered at the small picture and tried to match it with Jamar. He shoved it back. "You no play games with me! OUT!"

Jamar waved his blue bandanna in front of the Korean's face. "Know what THIS means?"

The man grabbed the bottles and jammed them under the counter. "Punk! You all punk! You think life hard! Go to hell, punk boy!"

Jamar felt blood burn his cheeks. "Don't you never call me no boy!"

The Korean grabbed the wall phone's receiver behind him. Jamar saw the man's finger stab the nine button. Then the one. Almost before he knew it, his own hand went to his pocket and gripped the .38. He brought it out, cocked it, and pointed it at the man's skull.

The Korean half turned, his finger poised to punch the

one again. Just as he did, Jamar fired twice. The man's body slammed against the rack of bottles behind him and slid out of sight to the floor. The receiver swung from its cord and banged against the wall. A faint voice asked, "Nine-one-one, may I help you?" Jamar shot the phone, then grabbed the bottles and ran.

Crack smoke was wafting from the Neon's open window. Jamar dashed to the car and shoved Zombie. "Get over shithead, I'm drivin!" Tossing the bottles in the back, Jamar jumped in the driver's seat and fired the engine. The car burned away.

Zombie put out his pipe and coughed smoke. He turned to Jamar. "Um . . . c-can I have another c-c-cookie?"

The minute Jamar opened his eyes, his head throbbed. The sunlight flowing through the window made him wince. He realized he was in someone else's bed, but it hurt too much to sit up. He smelled the clean white sheet and scented the sweet smell of a lady. With a groan, he rolled his head to see the peaceful ebony face of Ameeka on the pillow beside him. Jamar moaned and massaged his forehead with his fingertips. "Shit!"

Through aching eyes he scanned the room. It was small and shabby, but Ameeka kept it spotless. His clothes were scattered all over the floor. Cursing, he stood and stumbled to the bathroom. Grabbing both sides of the sink, he threw up. The sour stink of stale malt and puke drowned out the bathroom's usual scents of Ivory soap and Apple shampoo. Finally, Jamar splashed water on his face and rinsed his mouth out. He stumbled out to the couch, where Zombie lay sprawled on his back, one leg hanging off the side. Drool crusted his lips.

Jamar grabbed a pillow and whacked Zombie on the head. "Yo! Dust-brain! Wake up!"

Zombie yawned and sat up. When he realized it was Jamar, a huge smile formed on his face. "Hangover central, huh?"

"Oh, shut up. How come you ain't feelin sick?"

Zombie giggled. "Cause I only d-d-drank one forty!"

Jamar frowned. "How many did I drink?"

Zombie giggled again. "Three!"

"But I only took two."

"Ameeka had two in the fridge."

Ameeka stirred and opened her eyes before sitting up and giving Jamar a sleepy smile. "You feelin okay?"

Jamar scowled. "No! I feel like shit!"

Ameeka was seventeen, dark and pretty, with her hair in tight ringlets that defined her ebony face. She had a beautiful smile, but it faded as she sniffed the air. Her soft eyes went hard. "I told you I don't want no crack in my place, Jamar."

Jamar rubbed his eyes. "Oh, shut up. I'm tired of hearin you bitch all the time. You sound just like my ma!"

Ameeka slipped out of bed. "Maybe we tryin to tell you somethin." She glanced at the clock as she walked to the bathroom. "I got to get ready for work."

Jamar bent down to grab his jeans. "I wonder how many guys it gonna be today."

"That wasn't funny."

Jamar pulled his jeans on. "Wasn't sposed to be."

Ameeka stopped in the bathroom doorway, her nose wrinkling at the smell in the sink. "Couldn't you at least clean up your mess in here, boy?"

"I told you, don't rag me, bitch! An don't never call me boy! . . . You gonna make me an Zombie some breakfast 'fore you go?"

"There some eggs and bacon in the fridge, an a pan on the stove." Ameeka stepped into the bathroom and shut the door.

Jamar tugged his shoes on. "Yo! Zombie, can you cook?"

"S-sure."

"Then get your ass in the kitchen an make me some breakfast! An coffee too! You can smoke for dessert!"

Zombie went to the kitchen, moving like his name, but expertly loaded the Mr. Coffee coffee maker before snagging eggs and bacon from the fridge. "Um, want toast?"

Jamar pulled on his sweatshirt and slipped into his jacket. "Yeah. Toast. Lotta butter. So how we end up here?"

"Well, after y'all capped that Korean an g-got wasted off them f-forties . . ."

Jamar's eyes darted to the bathroom door. "Shhh, fool!" He walked unsteadily into the kitchen and lowered his voice. "So it really happen. I did cap the sucka, huh?"

Zombie cracked eggs in the frying pan and smiled. "D-duh!" He added bacon.

Jamar looked thoughtful. "Wonder if they got that shit on the news." He flopped down on the couch and flipped on the TV: TINY TOONS.

Ameeka emerged from the bathroom in her work clothes: a Mickey D's uniform. She headed for the door, but then stopped and came to the couch. "Jamar," she said softly. "I went to the clinic yesterday . . . I'm pregnant."

Jamar didn't look up from the TV. "So? Ain't my problem."

Ameeka put her hands to her hips. "The hell it ain't! You helped make it!"

Jamar stared at the cartoons. "How you know that?"

"You the only boy."

"How I know what you doin after that Mickey D's uniform come off? 'Sides, y'all shoulda been more careful."

Ameeka's eyes went hard as obsidian. "Look, you always tellin people you a man. Well, why don't you start actin like one? You just a boy! A LITTLE boy!"

Jamar shot up from the couch. His hand lashed out and whipped Ameeka's face.

Tears glistened in Ameeka's eyes and she touched her cheek. "I trusted you, Jamar. You said you were there for me! Be here for this baby!"

Jamar grunted. "I here for what 'tween your legs, ho!"

"Get out!"

Jamar grabbed a fistful of Ameeka's uniform and pulled her close. "Check yourself, bitch! I just done capped three suckas last night. I ain't afraid to do the same to you!" He smiled at the fear in Ameeka's eyes. "Now, that what bein a MAN about."

"Um," called Zombie. "B breakfas' ready, Jamar."

Jamar watched Ameeka walk silently out the front door. "Bring it here, shithead."

Jamar ate half his eggs and all his bacon. Zombie fired his pipe and filled the room with crack smoke. "Want me wash them d-d-dishes?"

Jamar stood. "The fuck for? C'mon! We cruise over to Razor's and tell him 'bout the drive-by."

They were just a few blocks from Ameeka's apartment when Jamar glanced in his rearview mirror. "There a muthafuckin Five-O followin us!"

"You do somethin wrong?" Zombie asked.

Jamar held the car at exactly twenty-five miles an hour, his eyes shifting from the mirror to the speedometer. "Do us both a favor . . ."

"I know, I know, s-shut up."

Jamar guided the car along the street. "Shit, they still behind us!" He flashed his signal and slowly turned left around the next corner. "Maybe somebody seen us leavin the liquor store last night . . . or doin the drive-by!" He gripped the steering wheel and again looked into the mirror. Suddenly he floored the gas. Tires squealed, and the Neon rocketed down the street. Instantly, the cruiser's lights flashed blue and red. The siren screamed to life. The cop car burned after the Neon. Jamar swerved the car around another corner, doing ninety. The back of the patrol car dropped and scraped the asphalt as it struggled to catch up. There was a traffic light at the next corner. It was red, and horns blasted as Jamar shot through without slowing. His eyes flicked to the mirror. "I gonna lose them fuckas! Just watch me!" Again, Jamar slammed the gas.

Suddenly Zombie's eyes went wide. His mouth opened, and the pipe fell to the floor. "Hey! Watch out for that truck!"

"SHIT!" Jamar slammed the brakes and twisted the steering wheel. The car skidded, then smashed head-on into the steel-plated nose of a garbage truck. Metal tore and twisted as the Neon's hood crumpled. The front wheels sheared off, spinning down the street. The truck's huge bumper cleavered the car's top. More glass smashed as Zombie was hurled through the windshield. He screamed as shards ripped his chest and face. His head crashed against the garbage truck's radiator. He finally hit the asphalt in a mess of glass and blood.

Dazed for a second, Jamar brushed bits of glass from his hair. Then he heard the approaching siren. He groped under his seat and found the Uzi, then kicked open his door and struggled out of the wreckage. The siren's scream hurt his ears. He saw the cruiser coming fast and fired the Uzi. Bullets pocked the cruiser's hood and cracked the windshield. "You fuckers killed my homeboy!" he screamed, and swung the gun to spray shots every-where. "You gonna deal with a MAN now!"

The cruiser skidded to a stop and the siren blipped off. Both doors flew open and the cops burst out. Taking cover behind the car's open doors, they ripped their guns from their holsters. They aimed double-handed as Jamar's bullets thunked the car's grille. Both cops fired. Jamar's body jerked. His back arched, and he crashed down to the concrete. His fingers twitched with a last bit of life before going still.

The cops waited for a moment, then approached the wreckage. One cop looked at what remained of the passenger seat and then down at Zombie. "Christ, what a mess." He holstered his pistol. "Should I call an ambulance?"

The second cop, a black man, was staring down at Jamar. He shook his head. "Just tell 'em to send the meat wagon." He turned away. "He wasn't a bad-looking boy."

The other cop took off his helmet and ran a hand through his brown hair. "Wonder what his problem was. Jesus, we were only gonna pull him over cause his buddy threw that cookie box out the window. Both of 'em killed for littering! That's going to make a hell of a report."

"LITTERING!?!" Jamar stared at the TV as the cops walked away from the demolished Neon, and the two words "THE END" filled the screen of the biggest television he'd ever seen. Then it faded to multicolored snow and white noise.

"What a stupid movie!" Jamar was so pissed it took him a second to realize where he was. Then another to stare around and realize he didn't know where he was at all. He was sitting on a bed in a small room. "Must be a hospital." But when he looked down at himself he saw no bullet holes or wounds. He frowned, seeing he was dressed in tight Levi's that only came to his ankles. White Adidas that were too tight cramped his feet, and a red break-dance-style leather jacket that was too small clung to his upper body.

He looked around. There was a dresser against one wall. The mirror, he saw, was half covered with Garbage Pail Kids and skateboard stickers, the way a kid would plaster them on. Jamar gazed in the mirror. The clothes made him look like a little boy, even though it was his own muscular body that filled them and his own eighteen-year-old face that stared back at him. There was something familiar about the clothes . . . And then he remembered he'd dressed this way when he was about eight. His frown deepened as he scanned the room: there was no other furniture except for the bed and dresser. The room was slightly bigger than a jail cell. There were no windows; only wallpaper with pictures of smiling dolphins on it. There were plenty of toys on the dresser; G.I. Joe action figures, a big box of Legos, and a big pink toy Uzi. Jamar looked up at the ceiling to see a light fixture in the shape of a clown, grinning down at him. The bed itself was small; a little boy's bed, neatly made with a Ninja Turtles bedspread.

"That it! I in a children's hospital!" Jamar suddenly felt the need for a drink, but there sure wouldn't be any forties or gin and juice in a children's hospital. At least a smoke? Jamar checked his pockets, but found only thirteen cents in pennies and nickels, a few pieces of bubble gum, a little jackknife, and a ball of lint. He rummaged through drawers; only coloring books and a pack of crayons . . . nothing but little-kid crap! Not even a pack of goddamn matches!

Jamar went to the door and twisted the shiny brass knob. Locked. He pounded and kicked. Finally, he put his ear to the door and listened for hospital noises or voices. But the only thing he heard besides his own breathing was the fizzing TV.

"SHIT!" yelled Jamar, kicking and throwing things around until the neat little room was a hell of a mess.

Finally, he sat down on the bed and peered at his watch. It seemed to have stopped, but still showed 8:13. He whacked the thing but the numbers never changed. An eternal 8:13.

Suddenly, the fizzing stopped and Jamar watched as words formed on the screen. Next showing at 8:13.

Jamar checked his wrist, and of course it was 8:13. He sank down on the bed and stared at the TV. It was all he could do. It came to life with the opening scene of what looked like one of those shitty made-for-TV movies; the ones with the childish plot and infantile acting and sugar-frosted morals. The title was BAD BOYZ. Jamar watched. Strangely, the beginning didn't come as much of a surprise . . .

"Jamar! How many times I gotta tell you! Clean up that room of yours!"

Somehow, Jamar knew that he would be watching reruns of that movie for a long time.

Trash Walks

Lucky sat on the faded red curb. He was dressed in ragged 501 jeans with rotting Cons on his feet. His eyes were icy pools of blue, and his long wavy blond hair almost reached his waist. His tan face was hard and looked old for fifteen. He was slender with a flat stomach and a thin chest. Ribs showed at his sides, but muscle had started to define his arms and chest. He was like a little tank worn from too many battles. The battered black backpack on the sidewalk beside him seemed to suit him naturally.

Lucky stood up and scuffed a shoe on the dirty concrete. In one motion he turned to face the old building behind him. Its brick was streaked with soot, and it looked like if the wind blew hard enough the whole thing would come down, joining most of the other buildings in the neighborhood. A wooden sign, spray-painted white, was nailed above the door: WEST OAKLAND RECOVERY CLINIC printed on it in red. Lucky sighed, looking at the building, and dug into his pocket. He brought out a rumpled gray T-shirt and held it out in front of him. It was grimy and torn and said THUNDER ROAD DRUG REHAB CENTER on the front.

"Drug rehab, my ass! I just got out that muthafucka an I still a basehead! Goddamn donkey show all that is!" Lucky balled the T-shirt up in his fist and flung it in the gutter before snagging his pack and stalking off down the street. Like the old saying went: "Trash walks."

A few hours later, Lucky sat in the wreckage of an abandoned building and watched the sun glow reddish orange through a hole in the rotted roof. He scanned the building. Broken glass was all over, and winos had left their marks. He opened the side flap of his pack, where a pouch of Top tobacco and a bag of crack waited. He spread the tobacco and the crack in the paper, then rolled it sloppy and fat. He fired it and sucked deep. Crack smoke swirled into the air, leaving a bittersweet tang that burned in his nose.

Lucky sucked smoke deep and long, holding it. The rock overpowered the tobacco, filling his mouth with a chemical taste. He always smoked his crack this way—crushing it into a powder and rolling it with tobacco.

The last shadows of evening were lengthening. Lucky let smoke trickle from his nose and took another drag. He lay down on the buckled concrete, pillowing his head in his arms. He closed his eyes and his mind drifted back to a few months before.

"Does this belong to you?" demanded Lucky's dad. He stood in the doorway of Lucky's bedroom, the Ziploc bag of crack dangling from his fingers. His clean-cut blond hair was mussed and his glasses were fogged, but he still looked pissed as hell. Lucky sat quiet on his bed, blond tangles of hair hiding his eyes.

His dad slammed a fist into the doorframe. "I asked you a question! Does this . . . TRASH belong to you?" He walked into the bedroom and grabbed Lucky by the T-shirt and yanked him close so their foreheads crashed. The man's gray eyes burned into Lucky's blue ones. "IS THIS YOURS? Answer me, boy!"

Lucky nodded.

"Goddamn you!" The man's fist clenched on the crack bag, almost busting it. He turned and hurled the crack out the window. "I paid a lot of my money, the money that puts clothes on your back and food on the table, to send you to Thunder Road. I believed them when they said you were sick! . . . And I trusted YOU when you said you were cured! This is your second day back home and you're still smoking!"

Lucky made a face. "Starin at a fuckin wall for five hours ain't gonna stop me from doin anythin!"

Lucky's mother peeked into the doorway. "No, Bill! They didn't cure my Lucky?"

The man's eyes burned with anger. "Your precious little Lucky is TRASH!" Cursing again, Lucky's father smacked the boy in the face with his fist. Lucky's head thunked against the wall, but he stayed silent. Lucky's dad yanked the dresser drawers open, flinging the boy's clothes to the floor. "Get your pack, get your sleeping bag, and GET OUT! You're a waste of my money!"

Lucky gathered his things and touched his lip, which had started to bleed. "Trash walks."

———

Lucky's eyes opened. The sun was gone and darkness filled the inside of the old building. The cigarette had gone out and the only sounds were from a few cars cruising the dimly lit streets. Lucky rolled another cigarette. The only light in his world was its glowing ember. Finally he stood and grabbed his pack. He spread his sleeping bag in a corner and pinched out his cigarette. Kicking off his Cons, Lucky slid into the bag and stared up at what passed for a sky.

He awoke the next morning to the sound of cars in the street. He rubbed his eyes and ruffled his hair, then checked his old Payless watch: 7:23. Pulling on his shoes, he stood up and rolled his sleeping bag. As he opened his backpack to stuff the sleeping bag in, he noticed that his crack was running low. THAT was something he had to do! He shrugged his pack on and walked out of the building to face the early-morning cold. The streets were empty, except for a few zombies who pushed shopping carts overflowing with cans.

Lucky's stomach growled as he walked past restaurants. He wanted food, but needed more concrete candy. Finally he went into a little coffee shop and bought a blueberry muffin and a coffee with money he'd earned panhandling. He made the coffee thick with cream and sugar until it went from black to a syrupy gold. Lucky was about to sit down at a table, but the clerk scowled and pointed a chubby finger to the door. Sighing, Lucky went

outside to eat as he walked. He was surprised to find he'd
returned to the abandoned building . . . maybe it was a
home now? MAYBE, but he still needed money for food and
crack . . . Well, he could probably do without food as
long as he had rock.

Sitting on a pile of trash, he took out his crack, tobacco, and papers. He expertly sprinkled a mound of tobacco in the paper and covered it with skull-white crack.
He lit the cigarette and took a huge hit. Crack was a
quick high but felt good. His heart beat like an engine
piston and his head spun. Smoke began to blanket his
brain like fog rolling in from the Bay. Suddenly, a thought
shot through the smoke, sharp and stark in his mind. WHY
DON'T YOU FIND YOURSELF A REAL JOB? Funny, that was
something his dad had said. I KNOW! I'LL BE A
GARBAGEMAN! Lucky sighed smoke and flicked away his
cigarette stub. Then he got his pack and left the building.
Maybe finding smart work would be as easy as finding
Dove, the dealer he scored from.

Dove sat in his coke-white Lexus at the entrance of
Mosswood Park. Lucky leaned against the car's door and
studied the other boy. Dove was like a bronze-colored
statue, polished and perfect. His nose was small, and his
lips looked like they'd been sculpted with care. He was
muscular and nineteen. His perm brushed his broad, shirtless shoulders, and his eyes were kept secret behind

black gangsta shades. A massive gold chain hung around his neck.

The warm midmorning breeze blew Lucky's long hair in his face, and he suddenly felt stupid standing next to the beautiful dealer boy.

"Yeah. I wanna work for you, Dove. Look, I'm out on the street . . ."

Dove grinned. "Save your stories, dude. I grew up in this hood. Just so happens I need me a runner. My other boy quit. All you gots to do is run the product to the little G-rats, collect the money, an bring it to me. It might be easy cause you white. You cool with it?"

Lucky smiled. "Cool." Then his grin faded. "Just cause I white don't mean I got things easy."

Dove studied Lucky. "You got some place to crib?"

Lucky shook his head. "I'm on the street, 'member?"

"Hop in. I got me a two-bedroom apartment deuce blocks over. Y'all can stay with me."

Lucky's face lit up. "Really? Shit, thanks, man." He threw his pack in the back, then popped the door and slid into the passenger seat. The leather squeaked and smelled new.

A few minutes later Lucky was stepping into Dove's apartment. It was like a palace; the walls were painted white, and white carpet covered all the floors. There was a big-screen TV, a kitchen with everything a kitchen should have, and two bedrooms with a bathroom in each. If anyone worked smart instead of hard, it had to be Dove.

Lucky ran to his bedroom, threw down his pack, and plopped on his king-size bed. "Whoa!" he called to Dove, who leaned in the doorway. "All this for me?"

"Duh. Maybe you live up to your name. Anythin else you need?"

"Um . . . got any beer?"

Dove chuckled. "Who don't in this hood? It in the fridge."

Lucky got up and went to the kitchen. He opened the double-door fridge. Food was piled on the shelves, and in the back were rows of Olde English and St. Ides forty-dogs. Lucky snagged a St. Ides and twisted off the cap. He threw his head back and chugged the malt. After slamming about half, he wiped his mouth, set the bottle on the countertop, and called to Dove, "Yo, man! You treat all your runners this way?"

Dove appeared in the kitchen, clad in an old half-tee and boxer shorts, holding a dumbbell weight in one golden hand. "Naw . . . but I never had a white dude workin for me." He grinned. "Could be a lucky move."

Taking the bottle with him, Lucky returned to his room, and then went into the baby-blue bathroom. He killed the rest of the malt as he slipped off his clothes and set the empty bottle on the toilet lid. Then he stepped into the shower and cranked on the faucets. He smiled as he smothered himself in Dove soap, and took time letting the water rinse it off. He scrubbed until the new soap bar was shaved thin. There was a full bottle of shampoo on the sink, and he spent about fifteen minutes washing his hair, which was streaked brown with dirt. Finally, he shut off the shower and stepped out. Water dripped on the tile floor. The towels on the rack were big and fluffy. It felt real good to be clean after months of no washing. Dry now, Lucky stood in front of the mirror and carefully brushed the tangles out of his hair with his old gap-toothed comb. He got a fresh shirt from his pack, but had to slip into his rotted jeans again. They were the only pair he had. Finally, he went into the living room, where Dove was buffing on a Soloflex and watching TV.

"So what you think?" Lucky asked.

Dove glanced over his shoulder and laughed. "You look a couple shades lighter than when I first seen you today . . . gonna need some new jeans, though. You can borrow a pair of mine for now."

Lucky smiled. "So, whattup?"

"Load the VCR. Scored a movie this mornin. DEAD PRESIDENTS. Wanna watch?"

"Sure . . . in a while, man. Got some stuff I gotta do first." Lucky went into his room and sat on the bed. He felt a little buzzed from the forty, but something was missing. He dug into his pack and rolled one of his usual cigarettes, then fired it and took a puff.

A few seconds later Dove burst into the room. "Nooo way, Lucky! I caught you slippin and I ain't havin that shit in here! That's rule numero uno! Yo, ever hear that old NWA song 'Dopeman'? 'Don't get high off your own supply'!"

Lucky looked up. "I . . . sorry, Dove. I just . . ."

"Just nuthin, what it is!" Dove snatched the cigarette from Lucky's mouth, the crack from his bed, and went to the window. He flung both things out.

"Déjà vu," muttered Lucky.

Dove turned. The scowl on his face faded. "Yo! Better get your head straight! You got a couple of runs. One dude hangs on Martin Luther King, an another on Perelta." He tossed Lucky a new black T-shirt. "Put this on. My last boy wore a black tee. That way the dudes know you with me."

Dove watched Lucky gather his things. "Yo! You got probs quittin your habit, I help you."

Lucky looked up from tying his shoes. "Why d'you wanna help me?"

Dove considered. "Don't know, Lucky." Then he smiled and laid a big-brother hand on Lucky's shoulder. "Maybe cause I like you."

"Well, thanks, Dove."

Dove left the room, but returned with a pouch full of crack bags and a Dogtown skateboard. "You can use my board . . . and remember rule numero uno!"

As Lucky left the apartment, he pulled on the black T-shirt and planted a shoe on the skateboard. He hadn't skated in a while, and it was pretty hard, but soon he got the hang of it again.

The dealer kid on Perelta wasn't hard to spot. He was a chubby Latino boy about eleven, and he stayed in the shadows of a shabby house. Lucky noticed he had a pink Bubble Beeper clipped to his baggy black SilverTabs. The boy smiled as drugs and money exchanged hands. Lucky stuffed the sweaty bills into his pocket. "Numero uno," he muttered.

"Huh?" said the kid.

"Um," said Lucky, about to skate away. "Don't you speak Mexican?"

"Shit no! I eat at Taco Bell, but that ain't 'cross the border!"

Lucky hit Martin Luther King and cruised along in the shadow of the BART tracks. A tall, wiry black boy stepped from a storefront doorway. He wore a Michael J. tee and carried a Roskopp skateboard. He had dark smudges under eyes that flicked from Lucky's black tee to his skateboard. "Dove?" he asked.

"Yeah," said Lucky.

The kid's mouth formed a half-smile as Lucky gave him the rest of the bags. Money materialized in the kid's hand. Lucky had turned to check the street as he took it, but when he looked back the kid had disappeared. Lucky frowned, then shrugged and skated back to Dove's apartment.

As he closed the door behind him, Lucky saw Dove kicked back on the black leather couch, watching rap videos and sipping from a bottle of Night Train. "So how was your run, homeboy?"

Lucky set the board by the door and wiped his face with his shirttail. "Okay," he panted. "I ain't skated . . . for a while . . . it's pretty hard . . . work." He went to the couch and handed Dove the money. Dove counted the bills quickly, then gave Lucky fifty dollars.

"Whoa, thanks, Dove!"

Dove shrugged. "You earned it." He took another swig of Train. "I got you a big jar of licorice. Chew a stick when you got the need for crack. It works."

"Well, I got a cravin right now."

Dove's eyes narrowed, and he gulped the last of the Train. "Yeah? Well, just remember what I said, Lucky. I ain't a kind boy like Bill Clinton. With me it TWO strikes an you out!"

Lucky's eyes saddened. "Um . . . you sayin I got one already?"

"Shit stink?" Then Dove smiled. "Aw, get out my face, white boy!"

Lucky grabbed another forty from the kitchen before going into his room. The licorice jar was on the bedside table. He took a stick and lay down on his bed to gnaw it. The licorice did help a little, but Lucky still wanted crack. But it was either smoke crack and be trash again or stop smoking and work for Dove.

"Dammit, Lucky! Wake up!"

Lucky blinked tired eyes to find Dove standing beside the bed. It was the first good sleep he'd had in months. "Whu . . . huh? Oh. Shit, what time is it?"

Dove checked his Rolex. "Almost nine, an you gots a run."

With a yawn, Lucky rolled out of bed and stood. His body felt stiff as he staggered over to the heap of clothes on the floor. He slid into his dirty jeans, pulled on his socks and Cons, then went into the bathroom and splashed cold water on his face. Dove was waiting in the living room with Lucky's pouch. Lucky shrugged into the black tee and took it. "Guess there no time for breakfast, huh?"

"Don't trip on it, man. There a Mickey D's on the way. You can afford it."

Lucky smiled, liking the sound of that. "Yeah! Guess you right. What streets today?"

"Castro, Adeline, Perelta again, an West Oakland BART. Oh, an take this. You gonna need it sometime in this hood."

Lucky took the black .45 Dove offered him. He held it cautiously, and just stared at the thing. He'd never shot one before, and this one looked toylike, but he'd seen enough guns in his fifteen years to know the difference between toys and reality.

Dove smiled. "Don't cap nobody 'less you gotta. I'd hate to see another dead brotha." Dove's glance went from Lucky's dirt-slimed jeans to his street-stained T-shirt. "When ya get back, I'll cruise you to Macy's in Frisco an score you some new threads."

Lucky's face brightened. "Really? You gonna take me all the way 'cross the Bay for some clothes?"

"Word." Dove smiled. "Can't have my new runner lookin like trash! 'Sides, be a good excuse to cruise the Lexus."

Lucky snagged the Dogtown and left the apartment. His muscles ached and sleep crusted his eyes but the need for crack kept him going. As he skated, his hand went to his pouch but he knew if he had even one cigarette Dove would have his ass. Lucky's leg muscles loosened as he kicked hard, driving himself from block to block. He glided on over to Perelta street. The little Latino kid was there. His stomach spilled out from under his shirt as he jammed Bubble Beeper gum into his mouth. Seeing Lucky, he stuffed the toy beeper into his pocket. As before, the exchange went fast: the kid got the crack, and Lucky skated off with the cash.

The dude on Adeline was about fourteen, and tall, with huge Nikes, big baggy shorts, and a Too Short tee. His hair was styled in a fade that needed trimming, and Lucky couldn't tell if his dusk coloring was natural or if he was just dirty. The kid traded Lucky a handful of cash for a half dozen crack bags. On Castro, the exchange was quick and easy. This was a REAL job!

Reaching the BART station, Lucky patted his pouch to make sure the gun was snug between the crack bags, then made his way through the mob of people waiting for their trains. There was a potbellied BART cop at the far end of the platform with a hungry-looking German shepherd. The dog's drool dripped on the concrete, and Lucky couldn't help giggling as the dog pissed, missing the cop's boot by inches. The cop swore and kicked the dog. Then Lucky wondered if the animal could pick up the crack scent in the air.

"Dove?"

Lucky turned to see a lanky white boy with red hair and brown eyes. The boy flashed a wad of half-hidden money. "Yeah."

"Well, hurry the fuck up! I ain't got all day," the red-head hissed.

Lucky only grinned, taking his time getting the crack. He was beginning to really like this job. Finally he dumped the last of the bags into the kid's eager hands. Suddenly, the boy spun around and ran!

"Hey!" yelled Lucky, before he could think. "Come back here with my money, fucker!"

Then a black-and-tan blur flashed past him, snarling. The cop had unleased his dog! People scurried around yelling as the roaring shepherd charged after the redhead kid. Lucky just stood dazed for a moment, then looked over his shoulder to see the cop running to catch up with his dog. Lucky wasn't sure if he was now on the kid's side or the dog's. But he saw the cop lumbering toward him, and in panic dashed after the dog.

"STOP!" the cop panted. Other people dashed for cover from the raging dog. Lucky saw the redhead disappear down the stairs that led to the street. The shepherd rammed into a fat black lady. She screamed and tore open her purse. Suddenly her hand whipped up and she shot the dog in the face with a mist of pepper spray. The dog yelped and clawed at his eyes.

Safe, Lucky thought as he stumbled down the stairs and onto the street. The red-haired kid was gone. Lucky cursed and tried to catch his breath, but decked and skated fast as the cop came puffing down the steps.

About an hour later, Lucky stood before Dove and handed him the money. "I, I got . . . jumped, man."

"WHAT!"

"The last dealer . . . the white kid! He just took the crack and ran! I tried to stop him, Dove! Trust me!"

Dove's eyes narrowed to icy slits, but as Lucky described what had happened, they warmed.

"Um," said Lucky at last. "You believe me, don't ya?"

Dove smiled. "Yeah. If you're lying, you're a damn good storyteller. I should have knowed better than to trust a goddamn white boy!"

"M-me?"

"Naw. Just watch for that shit next time!"

"Word, Dove!"

"Aw, let's you an me go shoppin for some dope threads!"

Lucky's face brightened. "Um, you mean it, Dove?"

Dove looked thoughtful. "I ALWAYS mean what I say!"

A short while later, Dove swung his Lexus into a space in front of Macy's clothing store in San Francisco. The sounds of the Dogg Pound cut off as Dove killed the car's engine. Then he and Lucky got out and walked into the store. It wasn't too crowded, and Lucky checked all the clothes with amazement. The clerk eyed Lucky's jeans, blackened with dirt, and his ragged Cons. She watched him carefully. A Def Leppard song screeched from speakers that hung on the wall. Lucky picked out six pairs of designer jeans and the same number of expensive T-shirts. He went to the counter, Dove following, and dumped the items in front of the clerk, who checked him again before totaling the cost on the cash register in a whirl of busy fingers.

"Three hundred fifty-three dollars and thirty-seven cents, please," said the clerk. "Will that be cash or charge?"

"Dead Presidents," said Dove, slapping four on the counter.

"Thanks, man," said Lucky. Dove just nodded.

The next morning, Lucky was up and dressed at eight. He stood before Dove in his stiff new clothes. "What streets today, Dove?"

Dove sipped from a big glass of OJ. "Only back to Adeline." Then a wide grin spread on his face. "An no more donkey shows with German shepherds an BART pigs!"

Lucky got his skateboard, pouch, and .45. He paused at the front door. "Um, how long will it take to pay you back?"

Dove reached for the TV remote. "Don't worry about it, man. You'll do it sooner or later . . . I trust you."

Lucky felt good as he reached the street. Damn, in only forty-eight hours he'd gone from being trash to a practically rich kid! He decked and skated toward Adeline. Shit, this's EASY . . . smart work! Another month and he'd be so rich he could be DOVE'S boss! Maybe he'd even cruise by his parents' house. Casually. Ask his dad how his job was going! Show him what "working smart" really meant! Trash might walk, but he could see 747s in his future! Let his fool of a father chew on that!

Now on Adeline street, Lucky scanned the block for a glimpse of a dealer boy. No one. He tailed his board into the doorway of an old factory building. The interior was caving concrete, and the air inside was damp and clammy and carried the scents of old piss and beer puke. All the windows were boarded up, no sunlight shone in. He entered the building, and squinted in the darkness. He stood there for a moment. Hell, Dove would never know! He walked to a corner and rolled one of his special cigarettes. He fired it and took a huge hit. There was a small sound behind him. He turned. "Yo? I'm Dove's . . ."

Suddenly, hands grabbed his shoulders and he was flung to the trash-strewn floor. A big Nike came out of nowhere and thudded into his ribs. Lucky gasped for breath, momentarily helpless. His pouch was snatched away! Running feet echoed in the building. Still gasping, Lucky rolled on his side and yanked out his gun. He tried to aim as a tall shape was silhouetted in the sunlit doorway for a second, but it vanished before he could fire. SHIT!

Lucky struggled to his feet and dropped his gun. He bent to pick it up but the pain in his side was sharp, so he ran for the doorway instead. He was just in time to see a black kid jump into a battered Buick lowrider. Tires squealed, and the car burned away from the curb.

Lucky ran into the street to try to chase the car, but he slipped in trash and fell to the asphalt. His heart pounded in his chest and his head swam from breathing the old car's exhaust. The fall had hurt his leg and he limped back into the building for Dove's Dogtown and the gun.

Dove was on the couch when Lucky returned. He was shirtless, a big beautiful bronze sculpture quietly smoking a Sherman. A bottle of Jack Daniel's fruit punch wine cooler rested in one brass hand, while the cigarette smoldered in the other.

"I . . . I got jumped again. They took it all! I tried to fight, but there were tons of 'em! They had bats, an knives! Musta been a gang or somethin!"

There was a strange sort of half-smile on Dove's face. He crushed out his Sherman in a gold ashtray and took a slow swallow of JD. "A gang," Dove cooed. "Mmm. Ain't that just like white folks. Blamin gangs for everythin that go wrong."

Lucky dropped the skateboard and approached the couch. "W-what do you mean?"

Dove's lips parted in a faint grin, and he shook his head. He snapped his fingers. Lucky's eyes went wide as a figure stepped out of his bedroom. It was the tall skinny boy from Adeline Street, and he had Lucky's pouch full of crack!

"This your 'gang,' Lucky?" Dove almost looked sad. "Thought you were smart, didn't you, man?" He took another sip of wine cooler. "Ya see, on every run you did I had a dude watchin you. There was one of my boys watchin at the BART station, and there was someone watchin you on your first day. Thought you could have one more little smoke, didn't you? Just 'cause I at the 'partment when you doin runs don't mean I can't see you."

"But . . . ."

Again Dove's fingers snapped. The thin boy handed him a .38 revolver. Dove loaded and cocked it. "You lied to me, Lucky."

"Please . . ."

Dove glanced at the thin boy. "Thanks, Shawn. You can go home now. You done real good."

Lucky's jaw quivered and tears burned in his eyes. He let them fall. He clenched his fists and frowned, trying to keep from sobbing.

"M-man, nobody ever gave a shit about me! I always been trash! Nobody ever trusted me."

"I tried," Dove said quietly. "I wouldn't had you watched today. If you'd done your job right. Trust is trust no matter where it come from. But you gotta EARN it."

"PLEASE! Gimme another chance, man!" Lucky pleaded.

Dove sighed. "How many chances you figure this world gonna give you?" Dove's face saddened again. Slowly, he raised the gun. "Trash walks."

Lucky's mouth opened. "How did you know . . ."

The gun fired.

Jungle Game

The two zookeepers slammed the panther into its cage. Both men were red-faced and sweating, wearing thick leather gloves and heavy protective vests, and big clubs held ready.

"This is the cat that got loose. Can you believe they found it runnin around Oakland!" chuckled one of the keepers. He wiped sweat off his forehead and stripped out of his vest. He was a mass of blubber with neatly cut gray hair and looked as if he'd been stuffed into his tan uniform.

The other keeper shed his own gloves and vest. He was almost as fat as his partner, with a stomach that hung out over his heavy black belt. "Talk about symbolism!" He mopped his face with a handkerchief and peered through the bars at the sleek midnight cat snarling back at him. "No wonder he was running around Oakland . . . he blends in just fine! Look at him, big, stupid, and black as the ace of spades! What was he doing when they finally caught him . . . rapping?"

The first keeper laughed while he clamped the big padlock on the cage door. "No. I think they found him standing in the welfare line holding a Mac-10!" He checked his watch. "Opening time. Let's grab a cup of coffee before all the kiddies come!"

The panther restlessly paced around the cage before lying down to watch people watch him.

Below the Foothills, in an old East Oakland apartment, Chad sat on his bed and looked up from a dog-eared ELF

QUEST comic. He was thirteen, and a deep, mysterious obsidian black. His body was at the awkward stage where muscle was just developing. He had a face that smiled easily and could change expressions in an instant. He had a small snub nose, and his eyes were a warm caramel color. His head was shaved, and hair had begun to grow back like sooty peach fuzz. He sighed and put down the comic. "It hot in here, an there nuthin to do."

A sloppily fat Hershey-brown boy, also thirteen, sat sprawled in a chair that seemed about ready to crack under his weight. Like the chair, he looked overstuffed in a faded E-40 T-shirt that stretched and strained over his chest and let his stomach spill out. He had a round friendly face, flat-nosed and wide-lipped, and his hair had grown out like an ebony puff. He was flipping through another one of Chad's comics while sipping from a half-full Coke can. He dropped the comic and pointed to the window. "Well, we could try hangin out there on the street, but I'm allergic to bullets. An I hate the sight of blood . . . 'specially when it mine!"

Chad grinned. "Yeah, Bobby? Well, I think all your paddin there could probably stop a few bullets, or at least slow 'em down."

Bobby took a last chug from his Coke. "Maybe. But I don't think I wanna find out!" He picked up another comic. "I spose we could skate to the zoo."

Chad snagged his scarred old Chris Miller skateboard. "Mmm. It would be cool to check out the animals . . ." He glanced out the window, looking past the ramshackle rooftops to the green Foothills. "But I never figured you want to skate UP to nowhere."

The fat boy smiled. "We can do like when we was kids. 'Member? I coast, an you skate behind me an push."

Chad spit out the window. "I think you way too big for that now, homey."

"Well, I hear they got actual breeze up in the hills, an nobody shoot at you. 'Sides, it somethin to do, ain't it?"

Chad pulled on his big tattered Filas. "So let's go to the zoo, man."

Bobby bent and grabbed his own dusty Adidas. "Cool. I think they got a new animal." He reconsidered. "Well, actually, 'cordin to the news, it that panther what got loose an was cruisin round here. Yo! Remember last night when I was sleepin over? Man, I knew I heard somethin growlin out there!"

Chad smiled, tying his shoes. "So did I, but I figured it was just your stomach."

Bobby made a face. "Bite me, fucka. Well, I never seen a real panther before . . . 'cept on TV."

Carrying his board, Chad walked to the door. "I ain't either. So c'mon then. Any zoo better than this one!"

The decaying brick-and-concrete jungle of the boys' neighborhood faded from their minds as they entered a

world of happy kids and fluffy animals: the Oakland Zoo.
Carrying their boards, Chad and Bobby walked among kids
of all colors: black, white, yellow, and brown.

"Look, Mommy! Elephant doody!" said a small chubby
white boy. His lips were crusted with cotton candy, and he
tugged on his mother's shirtsleeve.

"Hate to be the one who clean THAT up," muttered
Bobby. "Take a real big shovel!"

They watched a group of small black boys who were
obviously hood kids on some sort of field trip. The boys
had lagged behind the rest of their class and were gathered at the tiger area watching a pair of cubs prance
around their mother.

Chad and Bobby walked through the zoo. The day was
hot and sunny, but the Foothill breeze kept the tempera-
ture comfortable. They passed bears, monkeys, llamas,
and giraffes. Kids ran around everywhere, some paying
more attention to the popcorn and candy in their hands
than to the animals. The air carried the scents of many
things: people food from the snack bars, those little green
pellets fed to llamas, giraffe shit, and a loaded diaper as
a mother hurried toward the bathroom with her toddler.

Bobby changed course like an orbiting rocket, head-
ing for the snack bar. "I got me a five, gonna get some
popcorn. Want anythin, Chad?"

"Naw, I ain't hungry. Gonna walk over there."

Bobby joined the line at the snack bar, and Chad

walked across the pavement and around another row of cages. He watched a cougar roll onto its back, then moved on to the monkey cage. There was an echo of oohs and aahs from a group of white people who watched the monkeys beat their chests and do little dances. One of the men glanced at Chad, then chuckled to the woman next to him. "There's one that got out! Maybe it'll do tricks if we offer it a banana!"

The woman looked pissed and poked the guy in the ribs, but Chad felt blood burn his cheeks and quickly walked away. He caught sight of the same group of small boys who had been watching the tigers. They were hovering beside another cage. Right now they were the only other black people around, and Chad went over to be near them. But the kids were herded off again. Chad hesitated, not really wanting to follow a bunch of little boys. He wished Bobby would hurry up. He turned, and his caramel-colored eyes suddenly met a pair of lonely golden ones. He was standing face to face with a panther! The huge cat was the most beautiful thing he'd ever seen; sleek and muscular; and its midnight color was so deep that it almost gave off an ultraviolet glow. Tail twitching, ears half raised, the panther stood alert on massive paws. There seemed to be secrets in its golden eyes: calm secrets.

Chad stepped close until his chest pressed against

the rail in front of the cage. Even then he strained until his face almost touched the bars. The panther tilted its head and watched him. It seemed almost to smile. Again Chad's eyes locked with the panther's, and Chad couldn't look away.

" 'S up?"

Chad was startled and his eyes left the panther's to find Bobby at his side. The fat boy was grinning as usual, and his shirt had climbed the sloppy roll that passed as his stomach. "Sure you don't want any popcorn, Chad? It nice an buttery!"

"No. Um, check him out, man!"

Bobby munched popcorn and gave the panther a quick glance. "Yeah, I guess he pretty cool, but there some hella fine girls over by the alligators."

"Cool? For sure, but just . . . LOOK at him, man."

Bobby crammed his mouth with more popcorn and gave the panther a glance a little longer than the first. "He way cool. I checked how he was peepin ya out when I was walkin over. Like he likes ya or somethin. Y'know? Like a dog does?"

"It a lot more than that! An a lot different!"

Bobby smiled. "Oh. Then maybe I should leave you two alone for a while. Hey, wanna ride the gondola after?"

Chad scowled at Bobby, then his eyes traced over the

panther once more. "Gimme that pack of beef jerky you brung along."

Bobby dug into his pocket. "Figure he do tricks for meat?"

"No!" Chad snapped. He tore the cellophane off the jerky, then leaned over the rail and held the meat through the bars.

"Um," said Bobby. "That ain't such a good idea, Chad. Kitty got some sharp teeth!"

"Shut up," Chad muttered, not moving.

"But . . ."

The huge black cat met Chad's eyes for a moment longer before gently taking the jerky and walking to a shaded area of the cage to sit and eat all ten sticks.

"Whoa!" breathed Bobby, his eyes flicking from the panther to Chad. "Cooool!"

"Hey! No feeding the animals!"

Both boys turned to see a big blubbery man in a sweat-stained zookeeper's uniform standing behind them. He looked the boys up and down, then jabbed a plump finger at the sign on the rail. "Can't you read?"

Bobby raised a hand. "I can spell too. Potato. P-o-t-a-t-o."

The zookeeper made a disgusted sound.

Chad pointed across the walkway. "So why those kids feedin that baby llama?"

The keeper rolled his eyes. "That's the petting zoo! Those animals are THERE to be fed!"

Chad snorted. "Oh. So the panther ain't sposed to eat?"

The fat man's face got redder than it was already. "Don't get smart with me." Then he seemed to calm down and shot a glance at the panther, which had raised its head and was staring at him. "Just. Don't. Feed. The. Panther."

"Panther," Bobby began. "P-a-n-t-h-e-r."

"I'll be watching you two!" The man lumbered away.

Bobby snickered. "Yeah? Give me a Jackson an you can watch me do tricks!" He did a little jiggly dance like a hula.

The panther gave a funny-sounding chuckly cough.

"Stop that shit!" said Chad. "He'll throw our asses outta here!"

Bobby shrugged. "Well, I gonna get me a candy bar. You hungry yet?"

"No. Go ahead, man. I'll chill here."

As Bobby walked off, Chad leaned against the guard-rail and stared into the panther cage. The gondola went slowly along its cable, letting the people get a nice few of things from above.

Still lying down, the panther had finished the jerky. Slowly, it rose to its feet and came to the bars. Chad could almost touch its nose. Their eyes met and locked with sudden intensity. Chad seemed to shiver. His body went rigid. Like a movie out of focus, his vision swam in a blur of images. At first he couldn't make them out, but then the scene sharpened and he saw himself standing naked, surrounded by lush green plants and tall, vine-tangled trees. The picture blurred once more before clearing again. Chad saw himself running through a forest alongside the panther!

"Yo! Earth to Chad! Come in, Chad! Do you read me?"

The visions disappeared and Chad glanced around. Bobby stood in front of him. "Huh? What?" Chad rubbed his eyes.

Bobby smiled. "Hey, space cadet, you trippin?"

Chad looked at the panther, which seemed to be sleeping. "Aw, man! I was havin these . . . VISIONS! See, first I was standin in this African rain forest with all these trees an grass all around. Then me an the panther . . ."

Bobby squeezed Chad's shoulder. "I think you been readin too many ELF QUEST comics. You probably just took a little nappy-poo."

Chad frowned. "It wasn't no dream! . . . Least it SEEM real."

Bobby glanced at the cage. "Well, maybe it was your four-legged homeboy who was takin the nappy-poo."

"Huh?"

"Aw, c'mon, Chad. You been hangin around the animals too much. Let's motor. 'Sides, this place closin soon."

"We been here that long?"

"Naw. We just got here late, 'member? Now, c'mon before that keeper lock us both in a cage."

It was well after closing at the zoo. The sun sent rays of pink through the sky as it sank away, and the sounds of happy children were gone. A few figures moved along the walkways, cleaning up spilled sodas, scattered popcorn, and sticky candy wrappers. The second zookeeper came around the corner of the monkey house, pushing what looked like an ice-cream cart. "Hey, Richard," he called to his partner. "You fed the panther yet?"

The first keeper was also shoving a cart. The wild scent of meat trailed him. "Nope," he called back. Then he scowled and rammed the cart into the guardrail in front of the panther cage. "Don't see why I should. Some smart-mouthed little nigger boys already did. Too bad he didn't eat one of them. Probably taste better than this dog meat!"

The other keeper continued on to the lions. "Better lay off that language, Richard. This is a public place, y'know."

Richard spat on the concrete and opened the cart's top. "Gimme a break, John. The damn place is closed for today."

The second keeper shook his head and moved to another section of the zoo.

Richard pulled a red piece of meat from the cart and climbed over the guardrail. The panther leaped up, ears flat to its head and lips pulled back in a snarl. There was a warning growl from deep in its throat.

"Aw, shut up, you fur-faced Sambo," muttered Richard. He slipped the meat through the bars but pulled it back when the panther tried to take it, laughing when the cat roared. He threw a glance over his shoulder to make sure the cleaning crew had left the area. They were gone, and the other keeper was out of sight in the petting zoo.

"Stupid animal! Stupid black beast!" Yanking the wooden club from his belt, Richard rattled it across the bars, laughing once more when the panther roared in rage. Again, Richard stuck the meat through the bars. The panther charged at the food, but Richard's hand whipped it back out. The panther growled, and Richard whacked it on the cheek with the club. The cat stood on its hind legs and clawed at the bars. Richard swung the club again, hitting a paw. A third swing hit the panther in the face. Blood ran from its cheek.

Richard slipped the club back onto his belt with satisfaction. "That's right, BOY, bow down to your master! Stupid old spade!" He flung the meat into a corner of the cage and walked away.

Chad sat in a cage, knees hugged in arms and chin resting on them. He sat naked, like a Bushman, the panther lying beside him. Chad looked out through the bars as people stared at him and his night-colored companion. The people peered in with funny looks of curiosity. Chad turned to the panther. "Now I know what it like."

The huge cat seemed to smile. Its golden eyes met Chad's. "You already knew."

Chad looked thoughtful. "Yeah. Maybe I did."

Chad woke up in a sweat, even though the air wafting through the open window was chill. The ruby numbers on his bedside clock read 2:09. He looked down at Dubby, who was peacefully asleep on a mat next to his bed. Finally, Chad lay back again and closed his eyes.

The next morning Chad and Bobby sat in the living room, watching TV and eating from bowls of Cocoa Puffs.

". . . So, like I was sayin," said Chad. "I was havin visions of the motherland at the zoo. And last night I dreamed I was locked in a cage with the panther!"

Bright-colored cartoons flashed on the TV screen. Bobby giggled and gulped cereal. "Y'all tellin me you was Tarzan or somethin?"

"No! It wasn't like that. It was REAL!"

Bobby chugged the chocolaty milk in his bowl. "Real weird, you axin me!"

Chad clenched his fists. "Dammit!"

Bobby stared at his homey for a long time. "Okay, it was real. Um, you wanna cruise to the zoo again today?"

"Well . . . if it cool with you."

Bobby nodded. "Sho." Then he smiled. "Only, let's take the bus this time, okay?"

A short time later, the boys were again at the zoo. Chad headed straight for the panther cage. Bobby followed, but hesitated once, glancing at the snack bar.

The panther had been lying down, but when it saw Chad it got up and came to the bars. Chad slid his hand in and gently stroked the big cat's ebony fur. "Yo, Bobby. Check out his cheek! It been bleedin!"

Bobby leaned cautiously over the rail. "Yeah! Spose that Pillsbury Doughboy we seen yesterday been beatin on him?"

Chad scowled and glanced around. The zoo had just opened and there weren't a lot of people yet. "Sucka better not be!"

Bobby shrugged. "Or what? Ain't nobody gonna believe two little Oaktown nigga boys."

Chad sighed and nodded slowly. He watched the panther turn to a shaded corner of the cage and lick a paw. Chad stepped back from the rail and noticed a plaque next to it. He stood close to Bobby and began to read aloud: "Zaire is a African Black Panther. He was brought here from the rain forest in Kenya last year. He is fully grown. He eats"—Chad bent close and squinted at the plaque—"watermelon and fried chicken!"

Bobby's mouth dropped. "WHAT!"

Chad's hands went to his hips, and he spat at the plaque. "That what some asshole wrote on here with Magic Marker! Let's go ax Mr. Zookeeper what goin on!"

The big roly-poly man was standing by the goat pen, making notes on a clipboard, when the boys came over. He looked up at them and his face twisted in disgust.

Chad looked pissed as hell. "Yo, HO-mey!"

The man glanced quickly around, seeing no one else near. "What's your problem little . . . BOY! Lost your food stamps?"

Chad stepped to the man and poked a finger into his big soft stomach. "What you been doin to Zaire? He didn't have no cut on his cheek yesterday!"

The keeper shrugged and went back to his clipboard. "Panthers are dumb and clumsy! He probably tripped over his own paws!"

Chad's fists clenched. "Yeah? An I bet he wrote his dinner menu down on that plaque too!"

"Huh?"

Chad frowned. "WATERMELON AND FRIED CHICKEN!"

The man's face flushed crimson. "I don't know what you're talking about, boy."

Chad grabbed the edge of the clipboard. "You print awful sloppy, mister! Just like what on Zaire's plaque over there. Same color too!"

Face redder than ever, the man turned his back on the boys and began to waddle off. But then he spun around and looked at Chad with a strange sort of smile. "Watch it, kid! Sometimes animals go and die in a zoo . . . and nobody can find out exactly why!"

"FUCKA!" Chad screamed. But the man only laughed and continued walking.

Bobby touched Chad's arm. "Um, you wanna go back to the panther cage?"

Tears blurred Chad's vision and he wiped them fiercely. "No. Fuck this shit! I wanna go home!"

Back in Chad's apartment, the two homeys sat on the couch, not really watching daytime TV. Chad stayed silent. His mind kept returning to the panther. It wasn't only the panther's pain he felt; it was his own.

Chad suddenly sat up straight, his voice breaking through the TV's meaningless mutter. "I wanna free the panther!"

Bobby looked startled. "Huh? You crazy?"

"Maybe. So what? Ain't nobody care 'bout us or the panther! We all locked in cages!"

Bobby looked more puzzled than ever. "Huh?"

Chad changed the channel on the TV. "Them muthafuckas been beatin on him! An that lard-ass zookeeper practically told us he was gonna kill him."

"But WHY?"

"Goddammit! I don't know why! Maybe it cause he's just so black an . . . an . . ."

"Beautiful?" Bobby asked softly.

"Yeah. Maybe cause of that. White people killed off everythin else that been beautiful to us, an I don't want them to take Zaire too."

"YOU'RE beautiful, man. Sorta like the panther. I just a tub of lard!"

Chad smiled a little. "Well, you a beautiful tub of lard."

Bobby grinned. "Homo."

"Anyways, I goin tonight after closin. You comin?"

Bobby sighed and gazed at the TV. "Yeah."

The zoo always looked lonely at night after closing. All the people were gone, and the silence was only broken by the occasional sound of an animal moving restlessly in a cage. Richard slammed his cart into the guardrail and squeezed past, holding a bloody piece of meat. He glared through the panther's bars. "I made sure you were the last, Sambo!" he waved the meat. "Sorry your din-din got cold!"

The panther roared and sprang up. But Richard only laughed. He tossed the meat into the cage. The panther sniffed it and growled.

"What's the matter, Sambo? It's pure monkeyburger! Ain't that what you eat in Africa? I put somethin special in it tonight! Gonna taste real good!"

The panther lunged at the bars, golden eyes blazing like fire in the moonlight, but Richard was ready with his club. He hit the cat hard in the ribs. It whimpered and backed away into a dark corner. Richard chuckled. "Maybe we oughta rename you Rodney!" He walked off, the empty cart rattling. The panther sniffed the meat once more, but pushed it aside and lay down in the shadows.

Chad slept uneasily. He dreamed he was in a cage again, but alone this time. People stared in and poked him through the bars. Some threw rocks and bottles. There was a fat white man outside, dressed like a circus ring-master. He was grinning wildly and shouting things to the people, but Chad couldn't make out the words. A rock was thrown and slammed into his naked ribs. Suddenly, his cage door was flung open. The ringmaster's white-gloved hands grabbed Chad's ebony shoulder and shoved him to the dirt. The ringmaster ground his big boot into Chad's back. People swarmed around waving clubs and bottles. . . .

Chad woke and threw off his covers. He was sheened with sweat. He stood and shook Bobby awake on the mat. "Get up, man! It time!"

Both boys slipped into their clothes, grabbed their skateboards, then crept carefully through the apartment, trying not to wake Chad's mother. There was a crowbar in a bucket under the sink. Chad snagged it. The boys descended the stairs and made their way up the street toward the bus stop.

A while later they were standing at the entrance of the zoo. Except for a few lights inside, the place was dark and deserted. Somewhere a lion growled in its sleep. The boys moved away along a chain-link fence, leaving their boards hidden under a bush. Chad tossed the crowbar over, then they climbed. Chad made it in a matter of seconds, but Bobby kicked and struggled before dropping to the asphalt beside his friend. Chad scanned the scene. In the moonlight it was easy to see that the place was empty except for the restless animals. The boys walked warily side by side to the panther cage. Golden eyes glowed from behind the bars. The panther moved forward in sleek silence. It followed the boys as they walked around the cage to the door side, and only growled softly as Chad jammed the crowbar into the padlock. Chad pressed all his weight on it. The big lock squeaked, but hardly budged.

"Let me!" whispered Bobby.

Chad stepped back and watched Bobby charge, then body-slam the bar. The lock shook and squealed like a stabbed rat. "Um," Bobby whispered. "What you figure he gonna do when he free?"

Chad thought for a moment. "I don't know."

"Mmm," Bobby murmured. "Guess there only one way to find out." Again he levered down on the bar with his full weight. The cage door shook and the panther growled once more. Finally, the lock tore open and hit the ground with a metallic clatter.

"Yessss!" hissed Bobby, grinning.

Chad wrapped his arms around Bobby's jiggly middle. "Told ya you was a beautiful tub of lard!"

Bobby giggled. "Homo."

Both boys pulled open the heavy door, then backed away as the panther padded out into the silver moonlight. It looked around for a moment, then sniffed the air before moving toward Chad. Chad gave Bobby a glance, but the panther only nudged him and made a soft purr from its throat.

"Well," whispered Bobby, "go on an pet him, man, or whatever you do to say whattup to a cat bro."

Chad's hand trembled a little as he stroked the panther's smooth fur. The panther rubbed its head against Chad's hand and Chad scratched behind its ears. Bobby gulped, but slowly began stroking the panther too.

"FREEZE!"

Both boys and the panther suddenly found themselves surrounded by men in tan uniforms, all holding rifles. One of them was Richard. The panther's ears went back and its lips raised to reveal sharp teeth and long fangs. It used its muscled body to shield the boys. The men exchanged glances and raised their rifles.

Richard cleared his throat. "Okay, men! This is a dangerous situation we've got here! Fire at the count of three! One . . . two . . ."

"Nooo!" Chad leaped in front of the cat just as Richard fired his gun. The single shot echoed in the night. Other animals screamed from their cages. Chad clutched at his ribs and turned to Bobby, his expression confused. Then he took a step toward the panther before crumpling to the ground. The panther roared in rage and looked ready to leap at Richard, but instead moved to guard Chad. Chad groaned and rolled onto his back, pulling the dart from his side before going limp.

Bobby stared bewilderedly at Chad, then his own lips pulled back from his teeth and his usually friendly eyes went hard as stone. "You killed him!" he screamed at Richard.

The eyes of the other men shifted from Chad, who lay still on the concrete, to the fat zookeeper. Richard lowered his rifle. "It . . . it's only a tranquilizer. He's just asleep."

The other keeper dropped his gun and pushed past Richard. "The dosage was set for the panther, you fool, not a child! He could die!" He jabbed a finger at another man. "You! Get an ambulance!"

Richard stared at Chad's body and a sneer twisted his lips. "Little nigger had it comin," he muttered.

The other keeper whirled around. His chubby fist slammed into Richard's mouth. Richard stumbled back and wiped at the blood that was trickling down his chin. The other men began moving away. One turned and ran.

Another ran too. "They don't pay me enough for shit like this!"

The panther still stood over Chad, but also guarded Bobby. "Stay away, goddammit!" Bobby yelled. "If the panther don't kill ya, I will!"

Richard spat. "I'm gettin the hell outta here!"

The other keeper looked worried and took a step toward Chad, but the panther gave a warning growl.

"Stay away!" yelled Bobby.

Tears trickled down his cheeks. He stayed by Chad, whose eyes were closed and breathing labored. The panther pressed against Bobby, as if to give reassurance.

Bobby looked into the panther's golden eyes. What would happen to the beautiful black cat now? What if Chad died and the panther went back in its cage? Chad had talked about wanting it to live in Africa.

Minutes passed. The keeper stood helplessly, watching Bobby kneel by his friend. A siren wailed in the distance and Bobby shaded his eyes as headlights slashed the darkness. A shiny white ambulance pulled to a stop and the doors popped open. The attendants jumped out, grabbing a stretcher and running toward Chad. They stopped in uncertainty when the panther growled. Bobby stroked the panther and it calmed, allowing the men to lift Chad onto the stretcher. One picked up the dart and studied it, while the other checked Chad's pulse.

"Look, kid," the keeper said to Bobby. "This whole thing was a big mistake. You know that, don't you? What you witnessed here could bring down the whole zoo! No more lions, tigers, or bears for anyone to see."

Bobby looked down at Chad, then faced the man. "No animals for people like Richard to beat! This shit go on all the time, only there ain't a video camera or somebody who cares around to see it! You fuckas coulda killed him! What would you done if I hadn't been here?"

"It was an accident."

One of the paramedics looked up from attending to Chad. "Easy, son. This was a pretty big dose for someone his size, but he should be okay." The man picked up the stretcher and carried Chad to the ambulance. The panther almost moved to follow, but Bobby touched its shoulder.

The keeper eyed the big cat nervously, but then sighed. "Look, kid, I hate that bastard Richard as much as you. But there must be something we can do to keep this out of the news."

Bobby turned to the panther, meeting its calm golden gaze. Then he looked back up at the man. "Let the panther go free."

The keeper spread his palms. "What do you mean?"

"FREE. Like out of a cage forever." Bobby stroked the big cat's fur. "Be a damn shame if the zoo closes and there won't be any more animals to stare at."

The man held up a hand. "But HOW? You can't mean turn him loose!" He pointed toward the zoo fence. "Out there? How could he survive?"

Bobby's eyes saddened, gazing into the panther's once more, before looking past the fence toward East Oakland. "No, that ain't bein free. Not for none of us. That just a bigger cage. I want you to take the panther and set him free in Africa."

"I suppose that means you and your friend would want to go too?"

Bobby shook his head. "Maybe it a cage down there, but it the only home I got. I don't speak African no more. But the panther does. Chad heard him."

The man looked puzzled a moment, then considered. "Maybe something could be done . . ."

"Not maybe. Just do it!" Bobby watched the paramedics close the ambulance doors.

The keeper sighed. "The panther's been a lot of trouble since we bought him. He really hasn't been happy here."

"And one more thing," Bobby said. "Get that sucka Richard outta this zoo! People like him be why there problems like this in the first place."

The keeper smiled slightly. "THAT won't be a problem."

Blackbirder

Keeja sat back in his seat, lost in the beat of the drums. His eyes were half closed in a far-off gaze. The drumbeats got louder and louder until the whole school auditorium rocked with their rhythm. The man behind the drums was a dark, slender Nigerian. He was dressed in full African attire, a whirl of red, black, and green. As the drums went soft, he began to chant with the music, until the beat faded and silence filled the room. The man walked out from behind his big drums and bowed. There was a ripple of applause as he left the stage. The school principal stepped to the microphone. "Well, kids, its three o'clock, and that concludes our African-American Cultural Day presentation. Hope you liked it, and I'll see you tomorrow."

Chairs squeaked as kids got up and rushed out of the auditorium. But Keeja didn't move. He sat quiet, eyes still half closed.

"Yo! Keeja."

Keeja turned, blinking his eyes. Tarquin stood behind him, waiting. Fourteen, he wore long jean shorts and a "Dangerous Music" T-shirt. A black beanie that read "Oakland," gang style, rested low on his forehead. Tarquin was thin and smooth cocoa brown, with a little pug nose and full, pouty lips. "Shit, you really psyched over this African Day thing, huh?"

Keeja stood and shouldered his backpack. He was the same age as Tarquin, but gunmetal black. His nose was small, he had big front teeth, and his eyes were a dark coffee color. His body was wiry, but looked fragile and lost in his big soft jeans and hooded "Top Dawg" sweatshirt. "Well, didn't y'all like it?"

Tarquin made a face. "Well, course, man. But I ain't all caught up in that 'African roots' juba like you. Maaan, you so black you could come dope-fitted in leopard skin. UPS your ass to Kenya an you fit right in with our African brothas an sistahs!"

Keeja grinned. "Yeah, right back at ya, man. Maybe I just ain't been Europeanized like you."

Tarquin smiled and looked down at his clothes. "What you sayin? I bet they dressin just like me in Rwanda right this minute!"

Keeja looked thoughtful. "The last I heard they had a lot more to worry about than clothes. So, you comin over to do homework?"

"Naw, I comin over to watch big-screen TV. Y'all can do HO-mework!"

Five minutes later, Keeja and Tarquin stood at the bus stop in front of their school, Lincoln Junior High. It was a private school in the East Oakland hills, and Keeja's mother worked in the office to pay his tuition. Tarquin's mom taught English there.

A battered old bus snorted to a stop at the curb. The front doors opened and Tarquin and Keeja walked on. The bus driver was big, black, and grumpy. His elbows rested on the steering wheel, and the look on his face made it clear that he wasn't taking shit from any kids, either up here or down in the hood. Keeja and Tarquin flashed their passes and walked to the back row of seats. The old steel dinosaur squealed as the driver floored the gas and then bumped down the hill, where tar-paper roofs sent heat waves shimmering.

Finally, the bus swerved onto Foothill Boulevard, its big tires crunching through broken glass. Keeja pulled the cord hard. The driver scowled in the mirror, but swung the bus to the curb. The doors hissed open, and Keeja and Tarquin stepped off. The bus blasted into the lane, leaving the boys in a swirl of diesel smoke.

Keeja kicked a Night Train bottle into the gutter as the two homeys made their way to Keeja's apartment. "So what we got for homework tonight?"

Tarquin shrugged his backpack straps more securely on his shoulders. "Spanish an math. An not even a lot of it, cause of Afro Day."

Keeja nodded. "Kickin! Means I can finish my new model."

"Oh yeah. The Viper! So what color you gonna paint this one?"

"Well, 'structions say 'arrest me in red,' but I think I paint her silver, like on the old TV show, y'know?"

Tarquin grinned. "Cool. You good at chosin them car colors. That Mustang you done look slammin in bad-ass black!"

The boys talked more about model cars as they crossed the street and entered the crumbling concrete shell that contained Keeja's apartment. They climbed a flight of creaky box stairs and walked down a dimly lit hallway. Keeja unlocked a door, and the boys strolled into the apartment's front room. Immediately, Tarquin plopped down on the couch and grabbed the TV's remote. He clicked it on and settled back to watch ANIMANIACS. Keeja unpacked his books, laid a crumpled piece of binder paper on the coffee table, and then glanced at the TV. "Hope I can get this shit done 'fore ROCKO come on."

Tarquin watched his friend start on his schoolwork. "Aw, y'all gimme a guilty consciousnes, man," he muttered, and took out his own math book.

Keeja grinned and jotted words down on his paper. "You mean CONSCIENCE, homey."

"Speakin of which, how many more of those cultural days we gots?"

"I think African Cultural Day was the last one this year. Um, what the Spanish word for homework?"

"CAGA." Tarquin scribbled numbers on his sheet of paper. "Well, ax me, African Day was the best of all. 'Merican Indian Day was kinda cool too."

Keeja's pencil looped across his paper. "Um, what the Spanish word for bus driver?"

"Ours? EL GRUMPO GRANDE! So what you get for question number three on math?"

"I'm still on ESPAÑOL. NIACHE!"

"What that mean?"

"It Swahili for get out my face."

"Oh. Aw, what I see in you anyways?"

Keeja set down his pencil and smiled. "It a black thang. You wouldn't understand!"

Next morning at school, Keeja and Tarquin were loading their lockers with the day's books. Other kids, mostly white, were still scattered outside on the building's front steps. Even though Lincoln School claimed to be completely multicultural there were only a few blacks, Chicanos, and Asians.

Keeja and Tarquin snapped the padlocks on their lockers and headed up the hallway, pushing through the mob of kids to get to their classes. "I see you in history," Tarquin said, before opening a door marked "GYM." Keeja nodded to his friend and walked on. By the drinking fountain two white girls were talking. One was skinny and freckled with carrot-colored hair; the other was slim and bright-eyed with a pink ribbon to hold her long blond ponytail. Keeja supposed she looked pretty . . . if you liked the white idea of what that meant . . . but her voice always reminded him of a parrot with its tail feathers caught in a toaster. He almost gritted his teeth while walking past her, hearing her squawk to the other girl:

"I think we should have a European Cultural Day since we've had all these other ones for . . ." Her baby-blue eyes noticed Keeja. "MINORITIES. Don't you, Rebecca?"

The red-haired girl sighed quietly. "Yes, Amanda."

"Well," Amanda went on. "It's only FAIR. I mean, Europeans DISCOVERED this country! And they've done a LOT of good for it. Really, Rebecca, just think of what this country would have been today if the Europeans hadn't come!"

Keeja rolled his eyes and continued on. "It'd probably be a lot less polluted!"

Amanda didn't seem to hear Keeja's mutter. "Why shouldn't we learn about and be proud of OUR ancestors? Europeans have done so much GOOD throughout history. I'm going to speak to the principal about this. My parents are on the school board, you know?"

Rebecca sighed once more. "Everybody knows that, Amanda."

Going down the hall, Amanda entered the office and skipped past the secretary. She smiled a big bright smile as the principal came into the room.

"Mr. Schmit, I need to talk with you."

Mr. Schmit's smile was careful. "That's something you're real good at," he mumbled under his breath.

Amanda twirled her ponytail. "It's REALLY important. You see, Rebecca and I . . . You know, Rebecca Bronstein?"

Mr. Schmit checked his watch. "Yes, Amanda, but I really don't have time."

But Amanda went on. "We've been talking, and I think that since we've had Native American Cultural Day, Asian-American Cultural Day, Hispanic-American Cultural Day, and African-American Cultural Day . . ."

Mr. Schmit picked up a pencil and fiddled with it. "Yes, Amanda, we've certainly had a lot of Cultural Days this year."

"Yes, and I think now we should have a European Cultural Day. After all, don't you think we white children should learn about our roots and OUR many great contributions to the world?"

The principal snapped the pencil between his fingers and quickly tossed the pieces into the wastebasket. "Well, of course, Amanda. I'll certainly take this under consideration. But the Cultural Days here at Lincoln focus on minority groups. People who up until recently have been ignored or even oppressed by European-descended society."

Amanda looked shocked. "But I don't WANT to feel guilty about what people I don't even know have done to other people I don't even know. I just want to be happy all my life and not worry about problems that don't affect me."

A red vein popped up in the principal's forehead. He

glanced at the clock. "I'll give it some thought, Amanda. Now you better run along to class."

Amanda smiled from the doorway. "Thank you, Mr. Schmit. My parents are on the school board, you know?"

The principal clenched his fists until his knuckles turned white. "Yes, Amanda. I know."

He sighed, then picked up his coffee cup and walked next door to a smaller office. The assistant principal sat at his desk, eating a Big Mac and sipping coffee. He saw Mr. Schmit walk in the door and licked hamburger grease off his fingers. "Morning, Gil. What's up?"

The principal walked over to the Mr. Coffee and poured himself a cup. He sighed again and took a big gulp. "Oh, nothing."

The assistant principal took a sip of his own coffee and frowned. "Something on your mind, Gil?"

Mr. Schmit thought a moment. "Uh . . . what do you think about having a European Cultural Day?"

"Eh? Well, it's something I'D never think of." The assistant principal balled up his burger wrapper and made a hoop shot into the wastebasket. "But then I wouldn't have to, would I?"

Mr. Schmit sipped coffee. "Thanks! But really, Frank, what do you think of it?"

The other man shrugged. "I suppose it couldn't offend anyone. Just don't serve something like cupcakes as the special treats like we did on Gay and Lesbian Cultural Day."

Mr. Schmit still looked uncertain.

The assistant principal shrugged. "Well, you're the big chief here, Gil."

Mr. Schmit's face paled. "Please don't say that."

The other man smiled, then reached to a shelf and brought down a school history book. He flipped through the pages. "Well, Europeans do have a lot of history, good and bad. I guess it should be acknowledged. Maybe it is time we had a special day for the white children."

"Well, I guess that means we'll have a European Cultural Day," the principal said, rinsing out his coffee cup in the sink.

His assistant smiled slightly. "You're not looking too happy about it, Gil. How'd you come up with this idea anyway?"

"Amanda Teabrook suggested it."

"Hmm. Sounds like something she'd suggest. Her parents are on the school board, you know."

"I know," sighed Mr. Schmit.

It was the middle of the third period, and the principal was going into all the classes explaining the plan for European Cultural Day. Finally, he made his way into history class. Rowdy kids quieted as they saw him enter. Keeja and Tarquin sat next to each other in two small desks; the only black kids in the room. Amanda sat up front by the teacher's desk, and smiled her dazzling smile at Mr. Schmit as he began to speak.

"Class, it has been suggested that we have a European Cultural Day."

As if on cue, groans and sighs sounded throughout the room.

Mr. Schmit glared around, but began again. "As with all our Cultural Days, everyone will be required to make a speech, presentation, or project of some kind for display."

There were more groans.

Mr. Schmit cleared his throat and glanced at the teacher, who looked amused, then turned back to the class. "Now, students, just off the top of our heads, can you tell me some of the contributions Europeans have made to our country?"

The white kids just sank into their seats and glanced around, hoping not to be called on. Amanda's hand shot up, but the principal ignored her. His gaze shifted around the room, like a missile in search of a target. Finally, his eyes locked with Keeja's. "Keeja, how about you?"

Keeja's eyes widened. "Me? Um . . . I think they invented penicillin or somethin."

Amanda looked disgusted. "A FRENCH person did that!"

"Just who in the hell do you think Europeans are?" a brown-haired boy shouted.

Amanda glared at him. "Shut up, Pierre!" She thought a moment. "Well . . . well, they brought horses!"

"They got that idea from us!" yelled a brown girl.

Amanda sniffed. "Oh, quiet, Consuela!"

A multicolored mob of kids began to surround Amanda. She glanced around, looking desperate. "Well, um, they brought . . . pasta!"

A chubby Asian boy shoved Amanda. "We brought that! Haven't you ever had Cup O'Noodles?"

Amanda's face flushed pink. "What about American Indians? We gave them corn, pumpkins, squash . . ."

Tarquin sat on his desk and snorted. "Was that before or after y'all slaughtered 'em?"

Keeja smiled. "Shut up, man."

"EVERYBODY SHUT UP!" roared the principal. "Get back to your seats. Now! I've finished my announcement. European Cultural Day will be held on Friday of next week. Please inform and invite your parents. Start thinking about your presentations and projects." He stalked out of the room.

"So what you gonna do for this one?" Tarquin asked.

Keeja picked up his history book and stared at it. "I don't know. But this thing be FULL of white people, an I get some good ideas. Just gotta think about it for a while. Got any ideas of your own?"

Tarquin shrugged. "I probably do somethin havin to do with penicillin."

A dark-haired Jewish boy leaned over. "I know what I'D like to do. Stick Amanda in an oven!"

Keeja snorted. "Yeah, and you'd probably get to have a 'talk' with Steven Spielberg!"

Tarquin tapped the French boy on the shoulder. "Yo, Pierre, did I ever thank you for inventin french fries?"

After school, Keeja and Tarquin took the bus down from the hills as usual. The bus bumped through streets of cracked asphalt, passing shabby, burnt-out buildings that seemed to lean slightly in the afternoon sun.

"You gonna pull the cord today, or you want me to?" asked Tarquin, glancing out the window as the rusty old bus swung onto Foothill Boulevard.

Keeja shoved his history book into his backpack and sat relaxed in his seat. "Naw, let's ride downtown. I wanna check out the hobby shop."

"You need some more shit for your model?"

"Naw, I almost done with the Viper. I wanna check out some of the other ones."

A little while later, the two boys were walking into Howard's Hobby Shop on Broadway. The place was stocked wall to wall with models and scale train sets. Each section boasted a different type of model . . . cars, trucks, airplanes. Tarquin cocked his head as Keeja walked past the car section. "Yo, Keej, there's the Trans Am you was talkin 'bout last week!"

"I wanna try somethin different this time," Keeja murmured. He continued on into a section marked "Boats & Ships." He passed by shelves full of sailboats, submarines, yachts, and battleships. Then he stopped, scanning the sailboat shelf.

"You gonna build a BOAT?" Tarquin asked.

"No . . . a ship."

Tarquin looked puzzled but checked the row. "Here's a cool one."

"Naw, that a clipper ship. They didn't use those."

Tarquin looked even more puzzled. "Who didn't?"

Keeja didn't answer. Instead he grabbed a big box from atop the pile. "Mmm. HMS BOUNTY. Close to what I lookin for."

Tarquin held up a box. The boat on the front looked like something straight out of TREASURE ISLAND. "How 'bout this?"

Keeja looked at the model. "That still ain't right, man." He put the BOUNTY down and picked up another box, a little bigger and heavier. "This one perfect."

Tarquin looked. "Yo! That the USS CONSTITUTION! It in our book!"

Keeja smiled. "It a important part of European history. It a Revell too. They make good models."

"How much is it?" Tarquin asked.

Keeja checked the small pink price tag. "Ten bucks. An I got twelve."

Tarquin scanned the model paint aisle. You had to be eighteen to buy spray paint, and the nozzles were sold at the counter, but kids could buy the Testors paint in jars.

"The Testors on special," said Tarquin. "Three bottles for five bucks. I got a Lincoln on me. What colors you need for the ship?"

"Flat black, flat tan . . . copper for the bottom."

"Yo! Y'all tellin me them ships had copper bottoms?"

"They nailed copper on the bottom to keep worms from eatin the wood."

"Oh." Tarquin selected the colors that Keeja had said. "What about glue?"

"I got some at home."

Keeja with the model and Tarquin with the paint, the boys walked to the counter. The clerk bagged the items. "Sixteen-oh-five, please."

Keeja tossed her his money, and Tarquin added his five. Keeja looked a little worried. "Um, that all we got."

The clerk smiled. "Well, you're good customers. And it looks like something you'd build for school."

Keeja nodded.

"I'll let you slide until next time."

A half hour later, the boys were back in Keeja's apartment. They sat in his room, with model pieces spread out on the card table where Keeja did his work. By the closet were shelves of brick and board. They were filled with car and airplane models, and the whole room had a faint smell of plastic and Testors paint. Tarquin had his shoes and socks off and was sipping from a can of Coke while scanning the model's instruction sheet. Keeja was also barefoot, shirtless too, in the warm late-afternoon breeze sighing through the open window. He was undoing all the little pieces stuck on the plastic assembly trees. "This gonna be a bitch," he muttered.

Tarquin gulped Coke and burped. "Shit, you been buildin these things since before I even known you!"

"But this is fuckin level three! Super advanced, or somethin!"

Tarquin made a face. "Aw, you figure it out. You always do."

Keeja laid out the halves of the ship's hull. "Mmm. Gonna need new blades for my X-acto knife. Lotta cuttin to do . . . always is with Revells."

Tarquin crushed his empty soda can. "Well, I go score 'em for ya. Um, you gots any more money?"

"Yeah. I got ten more I been savin." Keeja bent and grabbed a dusty shoe box from under the table. Opening it, he handed Tarquin ten crisp dollar bills. Then he set one of the ship's hull halves upright on the table and stood a yellow plastic ruler against it. "Pretty small scale. While you at the shop, score me two packs of them H.O. train-set figures."

Tarquin tied his shoes and pocketed the money. "Huh?"

"You seen 'em afore. They go on train-set layouts . . . got women and kids too."

"Shit, Keej, you gonna have the best damn project of all! Buildin a ship that in our textbook, and puttin people in it. Gonna get your ass a A for sure!"

Keeja began to carefully dab glue on the inside of one hull half. "Oh, I don't know about that."

Almost an hour had passed before Tarquin returned with a pack of X-acto knife blades and two plastic pouches of train men. "Here you go, massa." He tossed them onto the table, where Keeja was carefully gluing the top deck onto the ship's hull.

"Thanks, boy," said Keeja. He laid the ship down on a piece of newspaper and picked up one of the train-people packs. He examined it carefully. "Just about the right size."

Tarquin bowed. "I was born to serve."

Keeja chuckled and began laying out the masts and spars. "Then get your ass over here and paint the hull down to the waterline."

Tarquin snagged another shoe box from under the table. Keeja had written "model-painting stuff" on the cover with Magic Marker. Tarquin rumaged through the box until he found a paintbrush. "Brown, right?"

Keeja fitted a new blade into the knife handle. "Um, no. Use the black."

"But the 'structions say brown. With white stripes."

Keeja grinned. "The 'structions wrote by white folks. Just use what I tell you."

Tarquin shrugged and reached for the bottle of black. "Well, you build models all the time. Guess you should know. Hey, want me start paintin the people after? That look like fun."

Keeja began trimming a mast. "Naw. I paint the people. Later."

Tarquin got a chair from the kitchen, then sat down and began painting the ship. "Y'know, we could turn in this project together. That way we both get A's."

Keeja started gluing a mast. "Well, I spose we could do that. If you REALLY sure you wanna."

"Well, course I am, Keej. I mean, look at this. It should be in a museum. Folks gonna really stop an check this out."

Keeja carefully put the ship down and thought a moment. "You got that right, homes!" He watched Tarquin paint. "You can even paint the people if you want. Now, listen up . . ."

———

It was Friday, European Cultural Day. Keeja and Tarquin hurried into the auditorium after leaving their project with the others, which were arranged on a table in the hall to be viewed by parents and teachers after the program was over. A few eyes turned to the boys, last to enter, as they took their seats near the back of the room. But everyone focused their attention on the stage as the principal gave a brief speech and introduced the first speaker. A polite round of applause rippled through the room but seemed to fade quickly as Amanda stepped to the mike. Faces in the audience winced when feedback screeched through the auditorium.

"Europeans are WONDERFUL people," Amanda began, and went on about how they had invented democracy and brought "proper" civilization to the world's less fortunate, primitive people, and how everywhere the Europeans went freedom, justice, and education followed.

Keeja whispered to Tarquin. "Maybe she's got this America mixed up with the one in that alternate universe!"

"Can you IMAGINE," Amanda went on, "what the Indians must have been thinking when the Pilgrims first landed on Plymouth Rock?"

"There go the neighborhood!" Tarquin muttered.

". . . and the AWE in the eyes of the poor African

Bushmen when the Europeans stepped upon their shores."

Keeja smiled slightly. "An said, 'Hey, boy, how'd ya like a free boat ride?'"

The audience squirmed in their seats as Amanda continued on . . . and on. Off to one side of the stage, the principal stared at his watch and turned to his assistant. "I never thought I'd say this, Frank, but I'm beginning to be ashamed of my color. I wish I could just shove her off the stage!"

"Well," the assistant began, "you planned this day for her. Can't you just politely tell her to shut up?"

The principal wiped sweat off his forehead with his shirtsleeve. "I'd like to politely wring her little neck! I mean, who does she think Europeans were? Little white angels? There's her parents, Fiona and Charles, right in the front row!" He made a face. "They're on the school board."

The assistant principal grinned. "I know."

But, finally, Amanda did finish her speech. The applause seemed a little uncertain, as if the people were wondering if they had really heard what they thought they had.

The principal shooed Amanda off the stage, and then spoke into the microphone. "Our next speaker is eighth-grader Shumba Brown."

Shumba, a chubby black boy, gave a short talk about

penicillin. The rest of the speeches went well, and just as the mostly white faces in the audience looked pleased with themselves, the principal stepped to the podium.

"Well, this concludes the oral part of our European Cultural Day presentation. Please join us in the school hall where the other students will present their projects. I'm told that Remi Latrelle has constructed an Eiffel Tower out of toothpicks, Consuela Cardoza has made a charcoal sketch of horses, and there are many other exciting projects. So please help yourselves to our refreshments—coffee, sparkling water, and bran muffins—then go into the hall. Thank you."

"Damn," Tarquin muttered, sipping from a glass of sparkling water. "I wanted some REAL European food! Like cheese sandwiches on white bread with mayonnaise!"

"C'mon," said Keeja. "Let's go see how the folks like our project. There's Amanda an her parents goin now."

Minutes later, everyone was in the hall, checking the projects. Oohs and aahs were heard throughout as the parents looked at their children's work. For extra credit, Amanda had made a picture of the Pilgrims and the Indians having dinner together. The crowd moved swiftly, commenting on all the displays.

Suddenly, a cup hit the floor and hot coffee splashed about. There was silence, and then a few gasps as everyone crowded around one corner of the display table.

"WHO IS RESPONSIBLE FOR THIS?!" the principal's voice boomed, breaking the silence.

"I'm absolutely appalled!" Amanda's mother shrieked. Then there was silence while everyone just stopped and stared.

Sitting on one corner of the display table was Keeja's ship. It was painted black, with masts standing tall and white cloth sails. A part of the ship's hull had been cut open, revealing hundreds of tiny brown people packed together inside like sardines. A few others were lying on deck amid blotches of bloody-red paint.

The principal was white-faced. "Keeja! Tarquin! Here! NOW!"

The boys came over to their project. The principal stood with his arms crossed over his chest. "Keeja! Explain the meaning of this."

Keeja glanced around. Faces of all colors looked uneasy. "I wonder about the meanin myself. A lot. But this a slave ship. A lot of white folks used to call 'em blackbirders."

"Why, that's the USS CONSTITUTION!" screamed Fiona. "It's a sacred symbol of our country . . . before this . . . this BOY disgraced it! He should be expelled!"

"Let Keeja finish," the principal said, frowning at Fiona.

Keeja began again. "Ships like this sailed to the coasts of Africa. The Europeans sent raiders inland to capture slaves." He pointed to the tiny people jammed together in the hull. "This is what they called a full pack. They could carry more people this way. In a half pack we had more room, but"—he faced Fiona—"your profits were smaller."

Keeja paused to gaze around the room again. The whole audience looked confused and angry. A few "Europeans" looked like they wanted to run. But no one moved.

Keeja began once more, pointing to the ship's deck. "The slaves were fed gruel, and were brought on deck once in a while. There they were able to dance and sing, but were made fun of and had hot water splashed on them by the ship's crew. This was sposed to pass as their 'exercise' and 'bath.' About three slaves died a day and were thrown overboard to be supper for sharks. Once the blackbirder reached America the slaves were unloaded in chains and sold to plantation owners. On the plantation they were forced to forget everythin about themselves and Africa. They had to learn European lifestyles and speak the white people's language." Keeja stopped and looked around at all the faces. "I guess that all I got to say. Me an Tarquin gonna leave the ship here. You folks can check it out if you want." Keeja glanced at Tarquin, who gave a short nod. "That's it for OUR European Cultural Day presentation."

The faces in the audience, even the black ones, looked slightly shocked. Amanda stood jammed between her parents, their faces bewildered and mouths hanging open. A rowdy murmur of voices broke the silence. Fiona slipped into her fur coat. "I can't BELIEVE this! It's NOT European history!" She turned to the principal. "Are you going to let them get away with this?"

The principal's own face reddened, but he gave Fiona a calm smile. "I know that this must be hard for you to believe . . ."

Keeja cut in. "HARD TO BELIEVE? It HAPPENED, didn't it? It sure ain't hard for ME to believe!"

"Just a minute, Keeja!" said the principal. He turned back to the audience. "As I was saying, I know this must be hard for you to believe but . . ." He faced Keeja for a moment. "But we must listen to these young men as we listen to all the other children and appreciate their project."

Fiona stormed for the door with her husband in tow. Amanda followed. "There's NOTHING here to appreciate!" Fiona snapped.

"Well, y'all saw SCHINDLER'S LIST and you 'appreciated' that!" muttered Tarquin.

A black man stood in the audience. He turned to the white mothers and fathers standing around. "Listen to Keeja! What he's sayin is the truth! We're always forced to listen to your version of history! Listen to OUR story for once!"

Shouting was heard throughout the room. The principal spread his palms. "Okay! Everyone please calm down! Help yourselves to more refreshments. This concludes the European Cultural Day presentation."

People began to quiet down and examine the projects again. Keeja and Tarquin stood at their display table. The principal approached them. "Keeja, Tarquin, I'd like to speak to both of you in my office first thing Monday." He left looking thoughtful.

Keeja and Tarquin just stood alone in the hall for a few minutes. Tarquin grinned and nudged his friend. "See, told ya we was gonna get a A."

ACKNOWLEDGMENTS

Much love to Bobby for having my back.
I always got yours.

Thanks to Howard Junker
for opening the door.

About the Author

Apollo was born in 1980. He started writing at age twelve, and at thirteen had his first story published in ZYZZYVA magazine. Apollo lives in Oakland.